"Someone is
And I think you know who it is."

"I don't!" she protested.

Seth studied her silently, his eyes cold. "We're dealing with a guy who sneaks around to do his dirty work. Someone who wants the world to see him one way, but who isn't what he seems. A charlatan. Sound familiar?"

She almost said it didn't, because no one in her present life was like that.

But there *was* someone from her past.

An upright citizen on the surface but as evil as they came where it counted the most.

Tessa stepped away from him, trying to clear her mind before she opened her mouth and changed her life forever.

"What are you thinking?" Seth asked. He could tell she was right on the edge of telling him something–something big.

"You just described my..."

"Your husband?"

Books by Shirlee McCoy

Love Inspired Suspense

Die Before Nightfall
Even in the Darkness
When Silence Falls
Little Girl Lost
Valley of Shadows
Stranger in the Shadows
Missing Persons
Lakeview Protector
*The Guardian's Mission
*The Protector's Promise
Cold Case Murder
*The Defender's Duty
†Running for Cover
Deadly Vows
†Running Scared

†Running Blind
Out of Time
†Lone Defender
†Private Eye Protector
The Lawman's Legacy
†Undercover Bodyguard
†Navy SEAL Rescuer
Tracking Justice
†Fugitive
†Defender for Hire

Love Inspired Single Title

Still Waters

*The Sinclair Brothers
†Heroes for Hire

SHIRLEE McCOY

has always loved making up stories. As a child, she daydreamed elaborate tales in which she was the heroine—gutsy, strong and invincible. Though she soon grew out of her superhero fantasies, her love for storytelling never diminished. She knew early that she wanted to write inspirational fiction, and she began writing her first novel when she was a teenager. Still, it wasn't until her third son was born that she truly began pursuing her dream of being published. Three years later, she sold her first book. Now a busy mother of five, Shirlee is a homeschooling mom by day and an inspirational author by night. She and her husband and children live in the Pacific Northwest and share their house with a dog, two cats and a bird. You can visit her website, www.shirleemccoy.com, or email her at shirlee@shirleemccoy.com.

DEFENDER
FOR HIRE

SHIRLEE MCCOY

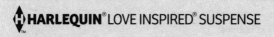
HARLEQUIN® LOVE INSPIRED® SUSPENSE

If you purchased this book without a cover you should be aware that this book is stolen property. It was reported as "unsold and destroyed" to the publisher, and neither the author nor the publisher has received any payment for this "stripped book."

PLEASE RECYCLE
THIS PRODUCT IS RECYCLABLE

Recycling programs
for this product may
not exist in your area.

™ LOVE INSPIRED BOOKS

ISBN-13: 978-0-373-44544-8

DEFENDER FOR HIRE

Copyright © 2013 by Shirlee McCoy

All rights reserved. Except for use in any review, the reproduction or utilization of this work in whole or in part in any form by any electronic, mechanical or other means, now known or hereafter invented, including xerography, photocopying and recording, or in any information storage or retrieval system, is forbidden without the written permission of the editorial office, Love Inspired Books, 233 Broadway, New York, NY 10279 U.S.A.

This is a work of fiction. Names, characters, places and incidents are either the product of the author's imagination or are used fictitiously, and any resemblance to actual persons, living or dead, business establishments, events or locales is entirely coincidental.

This edition published by arrangement with Love Inspired Books.

® and TM are trademarks of Love Inspired Books, used under license. Trademarks indicated with ® are registered in the United States Patent and Trademark Office, the Canadian Trade Marks Office and in other countries.

www.LoveInspiredBooks.com

Printed in U.S.A.

For nothing is hidden, except to be revealed; nor has anything been secret, but that it would come to light.
—*Mark* 4:22

To my family, because they know me well
and love me anyway.

ONE

Black.

Not the color of love, friendship, admiration.

The color of sorrow and death.

Tessa Camry lifted the single long-stemmed rose from the hood of her car and tossed it into her yard.

Five years.

Five black roses.

She glanced around the quiet neighborhood and saw nothing out of place. She never did. One rose every year to remind her. That was it. As if she needed anything to keep the memories from dying.

She slid into her Ford Mustang, backing down the long driveway, her skin crawling. Five towns. Five states. And still the flower had found her. She'd come to expect that it would, but that didn't mean she was happy about it.

"It's not like you went to a lot of effort to hide," she muttered, her words echoing hollowly in the car.

True. She hadn't been hiding, but she hadn't announced her location, either. No Christmas cards or phone calls—no contact with anyone from the past. Nothing to tie her to her college years, her married years.

The mission trip.

She shoved the thought away, checking her mirror several times as she made her way along the winding country road. Not a car in sight, but she couldn't shake the feeling that the person who had left the rose was following her; that the past was running toward her and one day it might catch hold and refuse to let go.

She shuddered as she pulled into the nearly empty parking lot of Centennial Physical Therapy. The small white building gleamed in the early morning sunlight. Tessa had been working there part-time as a physical therapist for five months. She didn't need the money—she needed the distraction.

And today, she needed it more than ever.

She jumped out of the car and jogged to the small reception area, the hair on the back of her neck standing on end. The memories were too close, and she wanted nothing more than to lose herself in her work. To forget what day it was, bury what had happened five years ago in flurry of activity that would exhaust her.

"Finally!" Dana Langtry looked up from the computer. Small and compact, her blond hair cropped short, Dana was energetic, efficient and friendly. She was also blunt and tough—a good combination for a physical therapist's assistant.

"I'm fifteen minutes early," Tessa pointed out as she went through the motions of shrugging out of her coat and pulling her hair into a ponytail, trying to pretend it was any other day rather than *the* day.

"Well, our first patient beat you by ten minutes." Dana handed Tessa a clipboard with the patient's chart.

"This is the new client that called last week, right?"

"Yes. I put him in room one." Dana glanced over her

shoulder, then leaned close. "And, just between you and me, I think he looks like trouble."

"How so?" Tessa asked absently, her heart still thumping too hard, her pulse thrumming in the aftermath of her frantic drive from home.

"Just a vibe that I'm getting." Dana lowered her voice a notch. "Too bad Sam isn't here. I'd rather he deal with the guy."

"I'll be fine, Dana." The last thing she needed was Sam Marne coming to the office to take a patient that he'd assigned to her. Sam had opened Centennial Physical Therapy five years ago and had slowly been building his clientele since then. The fact that he'd needed help at the same time that Tessa had wanted a part-time job had worked out well for both of them, and Tessa had no intention of messing with the arrangement.

"Probably, but I could just call Sam and—"

"It's his day off. If we call him in, he won't have any use for me, and I'll be out of a job." Tessa forced a smile as she glanced through the chart. Seth Sinclair. 34. Recovering from shoulder surgery.

"I still think we should call him," Dana huffed.

"I've been a physical therapist for a long time, and I've dealt with a lot of patients who look like trouble. There's no reason to call for backup," Tessa responded. "Besides, Darius Osborne referred the guy. He wouldn't have done it if he thought the man was a serial killer."

Darius, a childhood friend, was the reason Tessa had moved to Pine Bluff, Washington. She'd attended his wedding the year before and fallen in love with the area. After so many years of wandering, it had seemed like the perfect place to settle for good.

Now, it just felt like another pit stop.

"I didn't say he was a serial killer. I said he was trouble," Dana protested, glancing over her shoulder again. Obviously, the guy had her spooked, but Tessa had dealt with a lot worse than troublesome patients in her life.

"I'll holler if I need help," she joked as she walked down the narrow hall.

Her smile fell away as soon as she was out of Dana's sight. She didn't feel like joking. She felt like going home, packing her things and leaving town. She was tired of moving, though. Too many places, too many faces, all of it fuzzy and muddied by her constant need to outrun the past.

She wanted to put down roots, but maybe that dream—the one she'd been holding on to since her parents had passed away when she was ten—had died with Daniel.

She knocked on the door to room one, pushing it open without waiting for a response.

"Good morning—" She glanced at the chart as she stepped into the room. "Seth. I'm Tessa Camry."

"Ma'am." One gruff word, tinged with a hint of Southern charm.

She looked up from the chart into the most amazingly blue eyes she'd ever seen.

Seth's face didn't match his voice. There was no charm there, not even a hint of a smile. Just dark blond hair, those blue, blue eyes and a faint scar that ran from his ear to under his chin. Another scar edged his hairline, deep purple and much newer than the first one.

Dana had been right. He looked like trouble, but Tessa couldn't pinpoint why. Aside from the scars and the unusual color of his eyes, he was average—average build, average features, nondescript hair. Better than average muscle tone, though. She could see that in the corded strength of his shoulders and biceps.

She looked at the chart again. Better to focus on that than her new patient's bulging muscles.

"You're a friend of Darius's, right?" she asked, hoping she'd get more out of him than another *ma'am*.

"We're coworkers," he explained.

"So, you're in the private security sector?" She met his eyes and was shocked again by the vivid color of his irises.

"That's right."

"You work as a bodyguard?"

"I work as whatever my boss asks me to be. Until my shoulder heals, that's desk duty."

He didn't smile, but she had the distinct impression that he was amused—by her or the conversation or whatever situation had put him on desk duty.

She took a seat in one of two chairs next to the exam table and motioned for him to do the same. "I take it you'd like to get back to a more active job. Let's come up with a plan to make that happen."

"The sooner the better," he murmured, dropping into the other chair, his legs stretched out so that his feet were almost touching Tessa's.

She didn't shift away, but she wanted to. At first glance, she'd thought Seth was average, but the more she studied him, the more obvious it became that he was anything but that.

Maybe Dana had been right. Maybe he *was* going to be trouble.

She frowned, thumbing through his paperwork and reading the information he'd provided. There wasn't much. A shoulder injury that had required extensive surgery and therapy. A concussion. He'd marked a level seven pain in the affected shoulder and shaded a pain-point indicator through the shoulder and up into the neck, but he hadn't specified a cause for the injury.

"Were you in a car accident?" she asked, glancing up and straight into his eyes. Blue flecked with silver and rimmed with thick gold lashes.

"No."

"Sports injury?"

"No."

"I could spend the rest of the day guessing, or you could just tell me what happened and save us both some time."

He smiled, amusement flashing in his eyes.

"You know, Tessa, I think we're going to get along just fine," he said, leaning forward so that his elbows rested on his knees. "Here's the deal. I was in Afghanistan. My convoy was attacked and my shoulder got blown to bits. I came back to the States, had surgery and then rehabbed for a year."

"How long ago was that?" Tessa asked, making a production of taking notes because she didn't want to look in his eyes again. He was way more than she'd thought when she'd first seen him. Way more…interesting. Today of all days, she didn't want to notice.

Shouldn't notice.

"The first injury? Two years ago. I completed rehab a year ago and started working for Personal Securities Incorporated six months after that."

"When did the reinjury occur?"

"A couple of weeks ago. One of my clients was attacked, and I stepped in." He shrugged as if it hadn't been a big deal, but Tessa had a feeling it had.

"Did you have an X-ray or MRI?"

"Both. Everything is clear. My doctor thinks it's just pulled muscles and inflammation from old scar tissue."

"Let's check your range of motion. Go ahead and sit on the table."

He nodded, moving silently and easily, his white T-shirt skimming firm muscles and a flat abdomen. He wore black gym shorts and running shoes, and his left knee was crisscrossed with scars and swollen above the patella.

"Looks like your knee is bothering you, too."

"If we tried to fix all my problems, we'd be here for the rest of the day. How about we just concentrate on the shoulder?" His tone was easy, but there was an edge of steel in it.

"It's all connected. If one thing is out of alignment, the rest of the body suffers." She put a hand on his elbow, maneuvering his arm in the damaged socket. "Does this hurt?"

"Yes." He didn't wince, though, and there was no hint of pain in his voice or eyes.

"Mind if I take a look at the surgery scar?" She rolled up his sleeve, but could see only the edge of the scar, still deep purple and angry-looking.

"This doesn't look two years old."

"I've had two surgeries since the first one."

"You should have mentioned that before we started." She frowned and jotted a note in his file. "When was the last surgery?"

"Eight months ago."

"Your surgeon?"

"Guy on the East Coast." He offered the name, and she jotted that down, too.

"Okay. Let's work through a few exercises, see how far we can push things without making them worse."

"Sounds good." He flashed a smile.

Despite the quick grin, Tessa had the feeling that

Seth was assessing her. Whatever conclusions he was coming to, he kept them well hidden as she worked him through a series of exercises.

Thirty minutes later, sweat beaded his brow and his muscles were taut with effort, but he didn't say a word about pain or discomfort. He seemed determined to push through whatever he was feeling.

"That's good." Tessa put a hand on his arm, stopping him before he could begin another rep. "We don't want to overstress the joint or cause more pain than you're already in."

"I'm good."

"No, you're not. You're pushing too hard. That's only going to lengthen the recovery process. Lie down." She patted the exam table. "I'll have Dana come in and start some heat and stimulation while I print out exercises you can do at home."

"Anyone ever tell you that you're bossy?" Seth asked, standing up and stretching despite her instructions.

His question surprised a laugh out of her.

"More than one person. I took it as a compliment every time."

"This should be an interesting relationship, then." He used the hem of his shirt to wipe sweat from his brow and, without a smile, aimed his blue eyes straight at her. "I need to run. We can try heat and stim next time."

She didn't argue. Seth had to make the commitment to his recovery, and he had to be the one to follow through on it. "That's fine. I'll want to see you twice a week for at least a month. Why don't you set that up with Dana? I'll print out the exercises and meet you up front."

She tossed the words over her shoulder as she walked into the hall.

"Tessa!" Dana hurried toward her, a small package in her hand. "Are you finished?"

"Yes. I want to see him twice a week for the next few weeks. Can you set that up?"

"No problem. But, before I do, this was sitting on the reception desk when I got back from bringing Ms. Edna to room 3." She held up the package as if she'd just won the lottery.

"What's in it?" Tessa asked, impatient to move on to the next client. Like Seth, Edna was early, and that suited Tessa just fine. Keeping busy would keep the memories at bay, and she needed that.

"I don't know. It's addressed to you. Why don't you open it and find out?" Dana thrust the package into Tessa's hands, the brown paper packaging cool and a little rough. A white envelope was taped to the top, Tessa's name scrawled across it in bold black letters.

"So…" Dana leaned close, her eyes gleaming with excitement. "Who's it from? A boyfriend? A secret admirer?"

"No to both," Tessa responded, her gaze jumping to Seth's room. He stood in the open doorway, his good shoulder resting against the doorjamb, his arms crossed over his chest. Even his forearms were well muscled.

She pulled her gaze away, focusing on the package again. "I'll open it later. I need to print a couple of things for Seth. Set up his next few appointments, okay? Then run the sonogram on Edith's knee. We'll start her on the treadmill when you're finished."

She didn't wait for Dana's response, just hurried into Sam's oversize office. As a part-time employee, she didn't have her own space, but Sam had given her free use of his.

She set the package on his desk, doing her best to

ignore it as she booted up the computer and found the exercises she wanted to print. No one sent her packages. Getting one on the fifth anniversary of Daniel's death seemed…ominous.

She shut the thought down, jotting a few notes in Seth's file as the printer ran. Crisp winter sun poured in through the window behind her. But it couldn't warm the chill that filled her heart.

Five years, but she could still hear the wails of terrified children, still feel the blazing African sun, still smell the blood.

She gagged, stepping away from the desk and the package, and wishing she could step away from the memories.

Just then, the package moved, something inside of it scratching against the box. Tessa jumped back, knocked into a rock-hard chest and swung around, a scream dying on her lips as she looked into Seth's vivid-blue eyes.

"Careful."

Seth held his newest physical therapist's arm and looked into her misty-green eyes. Her skin had gone three shades of pale, and she looked as if she was about to jump out of her skin. Based on the way she was eyeing the package Dana had handed her, he'd say it had something to do with whatever was in it.

"You're supposed to be setting up appointments with Dana," she snapped, her eyes flashing with irritation and something else. Something that looked an awful lot like fear.

Leave it alone, his brain warned, but he'd never been all that good at taking orders.

"I already did. Now I need the printouts so I can

get on with my day." He touched the box, his curiosity piqued. "What's this?"

"A wrapped box," she responded dryly, grabbing a few pages from a printer and thrusting them toward him. "Here are the exercises. I'll see you next week."

Her dismissal couldn't have been more obvious, but Seth wasn't quite ready to go. Tessa and her mystery box were way more interesting than desk duty, and that's what he'd be heading for when he left her office.

He tucked the printouts into his coat pocket and lifted the box. It was light and just a little off balance, as if whatever was in it fit in one corner, leaving the rest of the space empty.

"Put that down," she said without looking away from her computer.

"You seem a little jumpy about it."

"It's nothing you need to worry about." She reached for the package, her fingers brushing the paper. Something skittered along the bottom of the box. Seth felt the movement through cardboard and paper. Tessa must have, too. She jerked her hand back.

He set the box down. "There's something alive in here."

Tessa made no move to lift it. "It seems that way."

"You don't know what it is?"

"No." She tucked a loose strand of deep red hair behind her ear and sighed. "Look, Seth, I don't want to be rude, but I have another patient waiting and—"

"Dana is in with her." He lifted the box again, examining the envelope taped to its top. "There's no return address. It's not even postmarked. Someone hand delivered it."

"You're probably right." Tessa didn't seem impressed by his deductive reasoning, and she didn't look happy that he hadn't left. She didn't reach for the box, though, and he thought that she'd be relieved if he took the initiative and looked inside.

"I spent a fair amount of time in the desert, and I've dealt with a lot of critters. Why don't you let me see what's in here? If it's something you don't want, I'll dispose of it."

"What if it's a snake?" she asked, hovering close to Seth's side. He could feel the heat of her arm through his coat sleeve, could smell a hint of vanilla in the air.

"The box isn't big enough. Besides, snakes don't skitter. They slide."

"How...comforting." She offered a brief smile, a dimple flashing in her left cheek.

"I don't mind snakes," he said, pulling the envelope from the box and handing it to Tessa. "It's scorpions I despise."

"I'll take a scorpion over a cobra any day of the week." She ripped the envelope open and pulled out a white note card.

"What's it say?"

"Today's date." She turned it over so that he could see the numbers scrawled in thick, black marker.

"Maybe there's a note in the box." He pulled out his utility knife and eased the tip under the wrapping paper. "Better tell me now if you don't want me to do this."

She remained silent, and he slid the knife blade under the box lid.

"What if it jumps out at you?" Tessa moved closer, her shoulder pressed against his arm.

His muscles tensed in response. Dormant memories sprang to life of a hundred moments spent with the only woman he'd ever loved.

He forced them away and flipped the box lid up. Better to look in the box than to look at the past.

"What is—"

Tessa's voice trailed off as two long, brown legs reached over the side of the box, the hairy exoskeleton as recognizable as it was surprising. Seth had seen his share of tarantulas. This one was bigger than most, its legs retreating as it scurried into a corner of its prison. A white envelope lay beneath it.

Seth reached to retrieve it, but Tessa grabbed his arm. "Just leave it."

"Don't you want to know who it's from?"

"It was sent to me by mistake."

"Your name was on the box."

"I'm sure there are plenty of people in the world with my name." She smiled, but her face had gone paper-white again, her eyes emerald against the pallor.

"You're scared."

"I don't like spiders any more than I like snakes."

"I don't think that's the reason." He shut the box lid, leaned his hip against the desk. "I think you should call the police, and let them know that this was sent to you."

"It's not illegal to give someone a tarantula." She rounded the desk, pulled masking tape from a drawer and taped down the box lid. "I'll take this guy to the pet store this afternoon. Someone will want it, right?" Her hands and voice were steady, and her expression neutral, but the fear in her eyes gave her away.

He took the box from her.

"I'll take care of it. See you next week, Tessa." He walked into the hallway, feeling the giant spider moving around inside the box in his hand.

Tessa didn't follow.

He wasn't surprised.

And he wouldn't be surprised if he showed up for his appointment next week and she wasn't there.

He knew all about having secrets.

Tessa could keep hers, but he was just curious enough to take a look at whatever lay at the bottom of the box. Tessa might not have wanted to know who'd sent it, but Seth did. Just in case the spider wasn't the last of the gifts.

Just in case there was trouble.

And generally, when it came to Seth's life, there usually was.

TWO

Go. Don't look back...

The words echoed through Tessa's mind as she ran up the steep hill that overlooked her house. Sweat slipped down her neck and pooled in the hollow of her throat, her breath heaving as she crested the rise and headed down the path that led to the Spokane River. Her dog, Bentley, panted along beside her, his muscular body relaxed, his one good ear upright. At nearly a hundred pounds, the huge mutt was large enough to discourage unwanted attention. He was also smart and alert enough to warn her of danger.

She'd chosen him for that and for his sweet, goofy ugliness. Long black fur over a homely face, one blue eye and one brown, he'd been abused by a previous owner but had still had the exuberance of a puppy when she'd found him at a shelter two years ago.

And now it was the five-year anniversary of Daniel's and Andrew's murders.

Don't look back.

But how could she not when everything she loved was in the past?

She picked up her pace, running until her muscles cramped and her body ached. Finally, she couldn't run another step and she pressed her elbows to her knees, trying to catch her breath.

Darkness had fallen, purple-black and thick. No moon. No streetlights. Just the Spokane River lapping softly at its banks and the distant lights of the city hinting at civilization. Dear God, how she wished she could find a place she could stay for longer than a few months or a year.

She straightened, a half-formed prayer nudging at the back of her mind, a cry from the heart that she didn't want to acknowledge. God hadn't answered her prayers five years ago, and she didn't expect Him to now. She didn't even want to bring her hopes and dreams before Him because she'd been devastated when He hadn't answered before, despondent when everything she'd ever cared about had been yanked away.

She couldn't lay the responsibility for that in God's hands, but she couldn't take it out of His hands, either. He could have changed things, could have saved her husband and brother-in-law or taken her with them.

She still didn't understand why He hadn't.

"Come on, Bentley. Let's go home," she said, hoping that her voice would chase away the melancholy mood. Every year, she got the rose. Every year she felt this way.

This year had been different, though.

This year, she'd gotten the spider.

Despite what she'd told Seth, she didn't think it had been sent by mistake. Someone knew that her brother-in-law had kept a pet tarantula when they were on mission to Kenya. Someone had wanted to remind her of that.

As if she needed any reminders.

Her legs trembled as she jogged back up the hill and into the deep woods that separated her from home.

Sweat cooled on her cheeks and she shivered. Early November, and the temperature was already in the thirties. This would be her first winter in eastern Washington. If she stayed.

Five years. Five towns.

Soon, it would be six, then seven and eight.

How many before she could finally stop running?

Bentley growled low in his throat, tugging furiously against the leash. It almost slipped from Tessa's grip, and she tightened her hold.

"What is it, Bentley?"

The dog growled again, his muscles taut, his body angled to the left. The night was silent and heavy, the woods and path still, but something whispered through the darkness, a quiet breath of movement that rustled the thick carpet of dry leaves.

"Hello?" Tessa called, her heart slamming against her ribs, her body numb with terror. She'd never felt as if she were in danger before—the roses had always seemed like a reminder of what would happen if she ever told the world the truth, which of course, she wouldn't. She had Daniel's legacy to protect. The work they'd done together, the children and villagers that they'd helped. She wouldn't risk those things.

Bentley let out a sharp warning, and she knew she'd better heed it. She pivoted away from the deep shadows, racing down the path toward home, Bentley lunging against her hold, snarling as he tried to get at whatever was coming up behind them.

Branches snapped, leaves crackled, feet pounded. Hers? Someone else's?

Pop!

Something whizzed through the darkness and Bentley yelped, stumbling. Tessa turned and saw something coming toward them. Black and broad against the navy sky, swooping in. She screamed, dropping the leash as Bentley snarled again and tried to run.

Another high pitched yelp, and then silence except for Tessa's ragged breaths and the thud of her pulse in her ears. Something slammed into her back and she fell hard, her hands and knees skidding across leaves and dirt, her mind sliding back five years. A tiny hut on the outskirts of a Kenyan village. Screams and terror and Daniel whispering for her to run.

She tried to shut it out, shut it off, force her mind and her body back to the present moment and the fight, but hands were around her throat, lips pressing close to her ear.

"I haven't forgotten. Have you?"

How could I? She wanted to ask, but she had no air, no thoughts. Blackness edged in, and she bucked against her captor, trying to use her weight to throw him off.

She had no strength.

Bentley snarled, the sound echoing in Tessa's ears.

Run! she wanted to shout. *Go home!*

Her attacker's hands tightened, then released. Gone. As if he had never been there at all.

Tessa wasn't sure if she was in the past or the present. In Africa or Pine Bluff. Didn't know if she was hurt or okay. Silence settled as thick as the darkness that pressed in all around her. She drifted in it, cold seeping through her clothes and settling in her bones.

Bentley whimpered, his nose nudging her cheek before he collapsed beside her.

She reached for him, her movements sluggish and uncoordinated. Warm fur, and something sticky and wet. Blood?

She had to get him home.

Had to call the police and get help.

First, she had to move.

She rolled to her side and pushed up to her knees, touching Bentley's silky head. "We need to get out of here."

She stood, her legs shaking, and Bentley struggled to his feet, huffing quietly in the darkness. He limped beside her as they maneuvered down the steep path.

She pulled out her cell phone and called 911, her voice raw as she explained the situation and gave her address. Her throat ached, her head pounded and she shivered with cold and fear, but Bentley was her first priority.

She disconnected, cutting the 911 operator off mid-sentence and dialing Bentley's veterinarian. Dr. Amy Spenser was almost as new to Pine Bluff as Tessa was. Neither of them had family or kids, and it had seemed natural to strike up a friendship. They'd gone shopping for furniture together, accepting that each had her secrets and a limit to how deep a connection she wanted to make.

"Hello?" Amy answered on the first ring, her voice soft and smooth with just a hint of an accent.

"It's Tessa. Bentley's been hurt." Tessa didn't have time for long explanations. Sirens were already blaring through the quiet night. Tessa's house loomed ahead, lights shining out from every window. Since Daniel's murder, she always left the lights on. Tonight, she was more than grateful for the habit.

"What happened?"

"I don't know. We were out on a run and someone attacked me. Bentley tried to help…" She recalled the pop and Bentley's whimper. Tried to make sense of it. "He may have been shot."

"Are *you* okay?"

"Yes."

"I'll be at your place in ten minutes." Amy hung up, and Tessa shoved the phone back into the pocket of her running vest.

"You'll be okay, boy," she murmured, more to reassure herself than Bentley. He limped beside her, slower than usual, but still moving.

That had to be a good sign.

Didn't it?

The woods opened out into her backyard, the long expanse of grass unobstructed by trees or shrubs. No sign of anyone lurking nearby, but her heart raced as she urged Bentley across the half-acre lot.

She rounded the side of the house and froze as Bentley barked.

A man sat in the old porch swing, his dark blond hair gleaming in the porch light, his scarred face familiar.

Seth Sinclair.

"What are you doing here?" she asked, taking a quick step back.

Seth watched Tessa back away from the porch and from him. The sirens he'd been hearing for the past few minutes grew louder, the sound blaring though the darkness.

"I brought the tarantula to the pet store." He held up the white envelope he'd come to deliver. "I thought you might want this."

"Just leave it on the swing." She eyed him warily, her hand clutching the leash of an oversize dog. Loose hair fell across her cheeks but didn't hide what looked like bruises on her neck.

Something was wrong. Very wrong.

Seth stood slowly, afraid if he moved too quickly,

she'd run. "What happened?" he asked, walking down the porch stairs, the sirens still screaming.

"We ran into some trouble in the woods."

Seth thought they'd run into more than "some trouble." Tessa's running pants were ripped at the knee, her vest covered with dead leaves. "You need to sit down before you fall down."

He touched her arm, and she jerked back, her eyes wide with fear. "Who gave you my address, Seth?"

"I asked around. It wasn't difficult to find you in a town this size." He took her arm as gently as he could and tried to urge her up the porch stairs, but she held her ground.

"You can go home. Bentley and I will be fine." She tugged at the dog's leash, calling to him as she tried to walk to the house.

The dog whined but refused to move.

"He's hurt," Seth pointed out, though he was sure that Tessa already knew it.

"The vet is on the way." Her voice sounded hollow, her face so white, he thought she might collapse.

He needed to get her inside, and he needed to do it now. He crouched next to the dog and let Bentley sniff his hand. He'd seen some homely mutts before, but Tessa's was about as ugly as they came. Ugly and huge.

"Come on, boy. Let's get you inside where it's safe." He slid his arms under the dog and was rewarded with a sloppy kiss that he would have wiped away if he'd had a free hand.

"You can't carry him. You'll hurt your shoulder," Tessa protested.

"It's already hurt," he grunted, the strain of the hundred-pound dog dragging at his injured arm. "And if you don't open the door so I can get inside now, it's going to hurt more."

She frowned, but ran to the door. Dirt clung to her pants and her down vest. Her elbow peeked through a rip in her long sleeved T-shirt, the skin raw and bleeding. She was worried about her dog's well-being—Seth was worried about *her*.

She ushered him through a large foyer and into a nearly empty living room. A dark brown couch stood against a wall and a rocking chair sat in front of a fireplace. A throw rug in muted greens and blues lay in the middle of the floor. No coffee table. No shelves. No books or magazines or photographs. A blank slate with cream-colored walls and dark wood trim.

"You can put him on the couch," Tessa said, her voice trembling. "He's bleeding. I really hope his vet gets here soon."

He placed the dog on the couch and took Tessa's arm. "Let's worry about you now, okay? Sit," he commanded, leading her to the rocking chair.

"The police—"

"I'll handle it," he cut in.

She leaned her head back against the rocking chair and closed her eyes.

"For the record," she murmured, "I'm not good at taking orders."

"I'm not ordering. I'm helping. But I'll keep that in mind for the future." He pulled a throw from the back of the rocking chair and tucked it around her. She still smelled like vanilla, under the musty aroma of earth, dead leaves and fear.

He shoved the envelope he'd brought her into his pocket and opened the front door, waiting impatiently as a police car pulled up in front of the house.

Seth knew the officer who got out of the car. Deputy Sheriff Logan Randal had a reputation for fairness and a drive for justice. Seth had worked with him on a few occasions, and he had a lot of respect for the guy.

"We got a call that someone was assaulted?" Randal asked as he approached the house, his eyes narrowing at Seth. "What are you doing here, Sinclair?"

"I know the home owner."

"You're the boyfriend?"

"No, he's not my boyfriend." Tessa edged in beside Seth, her shoulder brushing his arm. "Not that that has anything to do with what happened."

"It has a lot to do with it, ma'am. Most victims know their attacker." Randal moved forward, forcing them both to step back into the foyer.

"I didn't know mine," Tessa insisted.

"How about we sit down, and you can explain what happened?" Randal suggested. He placed a hand on Tessa's shoulder and led her down the wide hall.

Seth could have taken that has his cue to leave, but Randal would want to interview him when he finished with Tessa.

That was as good an excuse as any to follow them into a large kitchen. Like the living room, it was pristine and nearly empty, the walls light yellow, the cupboards bright white. A small round table sat in the center of the oversize room, four chairs positioned at perfect intervals around it.

Randal pulled one out for Tessa and motioned for her to sit, his gaze on Seth.

"If you want to go home, I can send an officer to your place," he suggested.

"I don't mind waiting." As a matter of fact, Seth was set on sticking around. He didn't know what had happened out in the woods, but it was obvious Tess was in trouble. It wasn't his problem, but if he could help out, he planned to.

"Then how about you wait in the living room or in your car? Another officer should be here shortly. He'll take your statement if I'm not finished with Tessa by then."

"How long will this take? My dog is injured, and I need to make sure he's seen by the vet," Tess cut in, her fingers tapping against the tabletop.

"You said the vet was on the way," Seth reminded her.

She nodded. "She is, but I don't want Bentley to injure himself more while he's waiting."

"I'll wait with him," Seth offered.

That would make Tessa and Randal happy. Seth wasn't so sure it would make *him* happy. He wanted to know what had happened to Tessa, and he wanted to know who to blame. Tessa had been quick to deny knowledge of her attacker, but that didn't mean she'd been attacked by a stranger.

He fingered the envelope, half tempted to toss it on the kitchen table and let Tessa explain who it was from and how it was possible that the tarantula and the attack weren't connected.

He'd wait, though. Give her a chance to tell Randal what she needed to. She was almost a stranger, after all, and he had no right to barge into her life and take control.

That's what his sister, Piper, would probably say. His three brothers would have a different view of the situation.

But Tessa's opinion was all that mattered. She'd tell the deputy sheriff what she needed to. With or without Seth's prodding.

He hoped.

The doorbell rang as he walked into the living room, and the front door swung open. A mousy brunette rushed inside. She glanced in Seth's direction, her gaze dropping to Bentley, who lay still and quiet on the sofa.

She hurried to the dog's side, putting her hand on his head, sliding it down toward an area on Bentley's haunch that was glossy and slick with blood. "Where's Tessa?"

"Speaking with the police."

"I'm Amy Spenser. Bentley's veterinarian." She opened the dog's mouth, examined his gums. "He's in shock. I'm going to have to take him to the clinic. Tessa!" she called, her attention focused on the dog, her dark eyes nearly hidden behind the thick lenses of her glasses.

"Right here." Tessa hurried into the room with Deputy Sheriff Randal right behind her.

Amy's gaze cut from one to the other, then settled on Tessa. "I'm going to take him to the clinic and start some fluids. You said you thought he was shot?"

"I heard a pop. Nothing like other gunfire I've heard, but I don't know what else it could have been." Tessa touched the dog's scruffy chin, her red hair sliding over her shoulder, nearly hiding the bruises on her neck.

"If it's a gunshot wound, the perpetrator might have used a silencer." Randal leaned over Bentley, touching the bloodied area. "We'll need the bullet if there is one."

"I'll keep it for you," the vet responded. "Right now, though, I need to get Bentley stabilized."

"I'll carry him out to your car," Tess said, patting the dog's big head, her hand trembling.

If he'd known her well, Seth would have taken her hand, tried to still the tremors.

"Let me," he said instead, sliding his arms under the dog and lifting him from the couch. The poor mutt didn't even whimper.

Cold wind knifed through Seth's jacket as he followed Dr. Spenser to an SUV and lowered Bentley into the back. The dog licked his hand, its tail thumping. No wonder Tessa had given him a home.

Seth closed the hatch, his shoulder throbbing. He'd been up since before dawn. After therapy, he'd dropped off Tessa's unwanted pet and then gone to the office where he poured over files until his neck cramped and his eyes crossed. He needed to go home and stretch the kinks out, maybe go for a run to clear his head. What he shouldn't do was get involved in Tessa's troubles. He'd been through six years of trouble. First Julia's death, then his injury, his surgery, his recovery. He didn't need or want anything more than what he'd finally achieved: normalcy, and a little peace.

He had a feeling that peace was the last thing he'd have if he didn't get in his truck and drive away.

Sometimes, though, peace was overrated. Sometimes God put a person in just the right place at just the right time to accomplish His will and plan. It could be that Seth had been dropped into Tessa's life at exactly the right moment to lend a hand.

He couldn't turn away from that. No matter how much he thought he should.

He shoved his hand in his pocket, his fingers brushing the envelope that had brought him to Tessa's house. He'd planned to deliver it to her, and that was exactly what he was going to do.

THREE

"You're sure that you don't know the perpetrator?" Deputy Sheriff Randal asked for what seemed like the thousandth time in the ten minutes since they'd returned to the kitchen.

Tessa wasn't sure what response he wanted, but apparently it wasn't the one she'd been giving. She gave it again, anyway, tapping her fingers against the stained wood of the old dinette table. "I never saw his face, Deputy—"

"Call me Logan. Most people around these parts do," he cut in, offering a quick smile that didn't meet his eyes.

"I don't know who attacked me. If I did, I'd tell you."

"Sometimes victims want to protect their attackers."

"I'm not protecting anyone." But in a way, that was exactly what she was doing. She was protecting Daniel, his legacy, his dream. *Their* dream.

She bit her lip, torn between the need to do that and the need to tell Logan everything that had happened in the woods—including the words that had been whispered in her ear.

"But, you *are* hiding something."

She was. That was the problem.

"I—"

The front door opened, cutting off the truth before Tessa could reveal it.

Logan cocked his head to the side and frowned, pushing away from the table, his hand dropping to his firearm. "Stay here. I'll see who that is."

Even if she'd wanted to, Tessa didn't have the energy to follow him from the room. Her neck hurt. Her head throbbed. Her elbow ached.

And she was more scared than she'd been in a long time.

She rubbed the bridge of her nose, closing her eyes and trying to imagine a scenario where the attack had nothing to do with her past.

I remember. Do you?

She did. Every moment of the nightmare that she'd survived and every bit of the secret she'd been charged with. Could she tell the sheriff about one without telling him about the other?

Footsteps sounded on the hardwood floor, masculine voices mixing with the quiet hum of the refrigerator. She wanted to say goodnight to Logan, climb in bed, close her eyes and pretend that everything was the same as it had been when she'd gotten up that morning. Unfortunately, that wouldn't solve her problems. She'd learned that the hard way, ignoring all the little hints that Andrew had let slip because she hadn't wanted to believe that he was anything other than upright and trustworthy.

It had cost her the only man she'd ever loved. It had cost Daniel his life. She couldn't let it cost any more.

She shoved away from the table, wishing she could push away the memories. She just wanted to forget and move on, but no matter how long or far she ran, she couldn't escape the past.

She grabbed the kettle from the 1920s stove and filled it with tap water. A cup of tea wouldn't sooth her nerves, but she needed to keep her hands busy, keep her mind occupied. If she didn't, she might sink back into the abyss she'd fallen into after Daniel's death. The dark well of grief and anger had nearly destroyed her. It had taken everything she'd had to pull herself out of it. Her faith had suffered, her relationship with God floundering as she wrestled with nightmares and fear. She couldn't allow herself to go back there.

"Tessa," Logan said as he walked back into the kitchen with Seth. "It seems like you left a little bit out of the story you told me."

"What's that?" she responded, reminding herself that Logan couldn't know what had been whispered in her ear. But that didn't stop her heart from thumping hard. One revelation would lead to another, and that was a path she wasn't sure she could take. Not without risking everything she and Daniel had worked for.

"The delivery you received this morning?" Logan prodded.

"It was nothing." She glanced at Seth, found that she couldn't drag her gaze away. He didn't look apologetic. But, then, she hadn't expected him to be that any more than she'd expected him to keep what had happened that morning to himself. She wanted to be angry, wanted to feel betrayed, but she'd have probably done the same if she'd been in his position.

"There aren't many people who would say that if they received a package with a giant spider in it," Logan said, pulling her attention back where it needed to be—on him, the conversation, the questions that she needed to answer. And, the ones she couldn't.

"I'm not most people."

"Apparently not, because most people would be happy to give me the information that I need in order to help them," Logan said as he settled into a chair.

"I *am* happy to give you the information. It's just... things are complicated." She turned away from the men and pulled mugs from the cupboard. "Would either of you like coffee or tea?"

"I'd rather have answers," Logan replied.

"Okay." She took a deep breath, willing her voice to remain steady as she pivoted, nearly bumping into the rock-solid wall of Seth's chest.

He stood just inches away, his coat open to reveal a blue button-down shirt tucked into black pants. He must have come from work to deliver the envelope.

"Do you want me to leave?" he asked quietly.

She almost told him that she did, but he'd gone out of his way to help her and she couldn't bring herself to send him away. "Whatever you want to do is fine."

She moved past him and sat across from Logan. "My husband was murdered five years ago today."

Logan stiffened, but he didn't speak.

Tessa knew he was waiting for her to continue, but she didn't know what else to say—how much to reveal, how much to keep hidden.

"I'm sorry, Tessa." Seth broke the silence, his tone gentle, his eyes the color of the sky at dusk—deep azure blue, and almost glowing in his tan face. There was something in those eyes, something that she'd lost so long ago she'd stopped believing she'd ever find it again.

She blinked, and whatever she thought she'd seen was gone.

"We were missionaries to Kenya," she said. "An insurgent group attacked the village we were ministering to. Twenty people were killed or wounded. Daniel was one of casualties. So was his brother, Andrew." Five years of recounting the tale had given her practice saying what needed to be said, but the words still made her throat raw and her chest tight.

"Why didn't you mention this before?" Logan jotted something in a small notebook.

"I didn't think it mattered." Didn't *want* to think it mattered, anyway. She pulled her hair from its ponytail and gathered it back in, keeping her hands busy so she didn't give herself away.

"Everything matters," Logan said, jotting something else in his notebook.

She needed to tell him everything.

She knew she did, but the words were stuck.

She cleared her throat. "Then I guess I should tell you that the guy who attacked me asked if I remembered."

Logan stilled, his face tight with irritation. "That's a big piece of information to leave out."

"She didn't leave it out," Seth responded before Tessa could. "She's telling you now."

Tessa didn't need his support, and she should have told him that. But the truth was, it had been years since anyone had stood in her corner, and even though she didn't want to admit it to herself, it felt good to have Seth there.

Plus, there were too many other things to worry about. Like trying to explain why she hadn't immediately told Logan about the whispered words.

"Everything happened so quickly," she murmured.

"I understand, but I need to know that I have all the details. Is there anything else I should know?" Logan looked up from the notebook.

Could she tell him about the roses?

Probably—the roses weren't part of her secret.

"Every year someone brings me a black rose on the anniversary of the massacre. It's been happening for five years, but there's never been anything else."

"Until today," Seth reminded her.

"Until today," she agreed.

"Did you get a rose today?" Logan asked, his expression grim and hard.

"I did. It was left on the hood of my car."

"Do you still have it?"

She shook her head, her eyes hot and gritty. She was saying too much, but she didn't know what else to do. "I threw it into the yard this morning."

"Left or right of the driveway?"

"Left."

"I'm going to see if I can find it, then I'm heading out onto the trail. Hopefully, I'll be able to collect some evidence. Stay put until I come back."

He strode from the room, his boots tapping on the hardwood floor. The front door opened, then closed.

Tessa went to the stove and lifted the kettle, pouring hot water into a mug and dunking a tea bag in it—and avoiding Seth's eyes. He leaned against the counter, his arms crossed, his hair a little windblown. He looked good, and that wasn't something she wanted to notice.

She yanked sugar from the cupboard and scooped two large spoonsful into her tea. "I appreciate your help tonight, Seth, but I don't want to take up more of your time."

"Is that a subtle dismissal?"

"I didn't think I was being subtle, but you're welcome to call it that."

"Touché." He laughed, his eyes crinkling at the corners. "But before I go, how about you tell me the rest of the story? I know you're holding back."

An image flashed through her mind—blood pouring over her hands as she tried to staunch the flow. Daniel's pale face and pale lips and dark, dark eyes. *It was worth it,* he'd whispered, and then he'd told her to go.

She closed her eyes, her head spinning.

Seth caught Tessa by the shoulders as she seemed to stumble forward. "You'd better sit down, Tessa."

"I'm okay," she said, but she didn't look okay to him. "I told Logan everything. There's nothing more to say."

Seth pulled the envelope from his pocket and handed it to Tessa. "You didn't tell him about this," he said.

He didn't think she'd look inside it. He probably wouldn't have if he were in her shoes. Not in front of someone else. And not if he knew it was somehow connected to his past.

She smoothed her fingers over the flap, her eyes dark and troubled. "*This* I really did forget about."

"Do you want to look inside before I give it to Randal?"

"I'd rather it just stay sealed."

"Why?"

"Because I've spent five years trying to escape the past, and whatever is in here will probably just tie me to it."

"Only you can do that, Tessa."

Tessa shrugged, a silky strand of hair escaping her ponytail. His fingers itched to brush it away.

He clenched his fists, surprised by the longing.

In the six years since Julia's death, he'd dated a few women, trying to fill the aching loneliness that losing her had left. It hadn't worked, and eventually he'd given up on the idea. He'd been happy with the decision, never doubting it even once.

Lately, though, he'd been yearning for the kind of connection that came from loving someone completely, from trusting her with every part of who he was.

"I guess I can't put this off forever," Tessa muttered.

Seth covered her hand before she could open the envelope. "Put these on first. We don't want to contaminate any evidence." He pulled leather gloves from his pocket and handed them to her.

"You've been carrying the envelope around all day. Do you really think there's going to be any evidence on it?" she asked, but she slid her hands into the gloves.

"I'm not worried about the outside. I want to protect what's inside."

She nodded, sliding her finger under the flap and carefully opening the envelope. She pulled out a photograph, stared at it for a moment, her expression unreadable. "What is it?" Seth asked, leaning over to get a look.

She shook her head and shoved the photo back into the envelope before he could get more than a glimpse of three people standing near a mud hut.

"Just another reminder of things I wish I could forget. Can you bring it to Logan?" she asked, taking off the gloves and sliding them across the table. He shoved them back into his pocket.

"Sure," he replied, taking the envelope she held out to him, his fingers brushing hers. A jolt of heat shot up his arm, that one touch reminding him of what he'd lost. What he'd told himself he'd never look for again.

Tessa's eyes widened and she pulled back, brushing her fingertips against her jeans as if that could somehow change what they'd both felt. "You should probably wait outside for Logan."

This time, he didn't ignore her dismissal.

He needed a little space, a little time to think about the reaction that he'd had to that simple touch.

He pulled a business card from his wallet and dropped it on the table. "I'll see you next week. If you need anything before then, give me a call."

"Thanks." She offered a half smile, flashing the dimple in her cheek. She was a beautiful woman. There was no doubt about that. But she had a boatload of baggage.

Not that Seth could point fingers—he had his fair share of baggage, too.

He walked outside, needing the cold night air to clear his head. Randal was nowhere in sight. Seth leaned against the porch railing to wait for him, the envelope and photo heavy in his hand.

It was none of his business.

He knew that.

But something in Tessa's eyes made him want to make it his business. Not the fear or the sadness, but the raw strength that he sensed had carried her through something terrible.

He slid the photo out of the envelope, careful to touch only the edges.

Tessa standing between two men. She looked young and carefree, a long blue dress covering her slim figure and a baseball hat shielding her eyes. Her hair was longer, the deep-red braid falling over her shoulder nearly to her waist. Behind her, a mud hut blocked the landscape, but it was obvious the picture had been taken in Africa.

Both men had black hair and tan skin. Both were tall and thin, but Tessa's gaze was on the older of the two, her smile only for him. He had to be her husband.

Seth flipped the photo over. No note, date or label.

He slid it back into the envelope, anxious to hear Randal's take on it. The photo had obviously been taken during the mission trip to Kenya. Whoever had taken it might also have put it in the box with the tarantula.

The wind knifed through his jacket as he went down the porch steps and around the side of the house. A light flashed in the woods at the back of Tessa's property— Randal, searching for evidence.

Seth could sit in his car and wait for him to return, but he didn't believe in standing still when he could be moving forward. Something in Tessa's past had come for her. The sooner Randal figured out what it was, the safer she would be.

And that's the way Seth wanted her to be. Safe.

The word ricocheted through him, a grim reminder of his failures.

He hadn't been able to keep Julia safe.

He'd been in Afghanistan when she'd been killed by a drunk driver. He'd flown home to arrange her funeral, to comfort her parents and his, to try to come to terms with the fact that his best friend—his childhood sweetheart, the woman he'd married straight out of college—was gone, and there was nothing he could do to change it.

He'd thrown himself into military life after that, making a career out of working covert operations deep in enemy territory. He'd planned to keep doing that until retirement, because work numbed the loss.

But God had had other plans, and Seth had been forced to leave the military much earlier than he'd expected. He couldn't complain. He'd survived his injuries, had found a new career, created a life that kept him content and happy.

But guilt about Julia tormented him every day. And there was no getting around that.

He tucked the envelope into his pocket and headed across the dark yard. There was no way he would leave Tessa alone until he made sure that everything was in place to protect her.

FOUR

Tessa hated silence—her mind filled it with voices from the past. Daniel's. Andrew's. The dozen children she'd been teaching the night of the attack.

If she hadn't been at the church with them, she'd have died in the tiny hut that she and Daniel shared. The one they had been standing in front of in the photograph.

She shuddered.

She vividly remembered the day the photo had been taken. They'd been in Kenya for three days and had two years of work stretching out ahead of them. A villager had taken the photo. Tessa hadn't seen it since the massacre.

She flicked on the small radio that sat on the kitchen counter, letting classical music drift into the silence. Better, but not the same as having Bentley following behind her as she paced to the window that looked out over the backyard.

Amy should be calling with an update soon. If she didn't, Tessa would call her. Bentley was the closest thing to family that she had, and she wanted to know that he was going to be okay.

She frowned, tucking Seth's business card into the junk drawer beside the fridge. She had no intention of calling *him*. He was too much of everything that she didn't want in her life. Confident, decisive and driven, he was probably the kind of person who devoted time and attention and complete commitment to whatever cause he was championing. Right now, he seemed to be championing her, and that felt too good, the temptation to lean on him and let him take care of things for her almost overwhelming her common sense.

Almost?

Completely.

She'd given him the photo and asked him to bring it to Logan. As if getting it out of the house could change the fact that she'd received it.

A light bobbed on the hill, appearing and disappearing as someone moved through the trees. Probably Logan. If Tessa had been brave enough, she'd have joined him. It would have been easy to pinpoint the place where she'd been attacked, show him the direction the attacker had come from.

She turned away from the backyard, her chest tight, her eyes hot. She'd dreamed big when she was in college, imagining a life that was exactly the opposite of the one she'd had growing up. Security and routine, love and happiness. She thought she'd have it all with Daniel, and she almost had.

Instead, she'd come full circle, ending up right back where she'd been when her parents had died and she'd been shipped off to foster care.

Alone and terrified.

She shoved the thought away. She was alone by choice, because relationships were too complicated and too risky. She liked her old Victorian house and her job, and loved the serenity and slow pace of Pine Bluff, Washington.

The bruises on her throat throbbed.

She didn't want to leave Pine Bluff, but she wasn't sure she could stay.

Walking up the curved staircase, she ran her hand over the smooth mahogany banister. She'd spent days stripping paint off the hand-carved wood and polishing the intricate spindles, imagining the generations of people who had walked up and down the stairs, trailing their hands along the railing. She'd planned to become part of the house's history.

Her plans were changing.

She might not want deep connections and all the complications that went with them, but she wanted a life lived in peace without the past making constant appearances.

Maybe that meant doing what she'd considered doing dozens of times since the first rose had arrived— changing her name, becoming someone completely new. People went into hiding all the time, created wonderful new lives out of the ashes of their old ones.

In her room overlooking the backyard, she pulled back the gauzy curtains and stared up at the hill behind the house. The light was gone. Either Logan had finished his search, or he'd crested the rise and was heading down toward the river.

He'd want to talk to her when he returned, but for now, she needed keep her mind occupied and her hands busy. She lifted the phone that sat on the nightstand and dialed Amy's number. She'd check on Bentley, and then she'd go up to the attic and grab the suitcase she'd put there when she'd moved in.

Never again, she'd told herself. *No more packing and unpacking and packing again. This is it forever.*

She should have known things wouldn't work out

that way. Should have kept the suitcase under her bed like she had for the first four years she'd been back in the States.

She left a message on Amy's voicemail and walked down the hall to the attic door. The old-fashioned glass doorknob gleamed in the overhead light, the skeleton key that was usually in the small nook on the wall beside the door already in the keyhole.

Had she left the key there the last time she'd gone in the attic? When had that been? A week ago? More?

Wouldn't she have already noticed the key in keyhole if it had been there since the last time she used it?

Of course she would have. She'd spent the past five years noticing everything, constantly on the alert, tracking changes in her environment and looking for any sign that danger was closing in.

She hadn't left the key in the hole. Someone else had.

Her heart jumped, her throat dry with fear. Someone could be in the house. Her attacker could be waiting in the attic for her to settle down and go to sleep.

She backed away from the door, her pulse pounding frantically.

The doorbell rang and she screamed, whirling away from the attic, then turning back, afraid if she wasn't watching the doorknob, it would start to turn.

The doorbell rang again and the front door opened, cold air gusting in.

"Tessa?" Seth called from the foyer.

"Upstairs," she responded, her voice gritty with fear. Footsteps pounded on the stairs and Seth appeared on the landing, his hair mussed from the wind, his eyes glowing deep blue.

"I thought you'd left," she said, more relieved than she wanted to be that he hadn't.

"I gave Randal the picture and I thought I'd check in with you one more time before I went home," he responded. "What's wrong?"

She gestured to the doorknob and key. "Someone has been in the attic."

"You're sure?" He moved past her, the comforting scent of pine needles and winter air filling the wide hall.

Was she? With Seth there, she suddenly wasn't sure that she *was* in danger. Did she *really* know that *she* hadn't left the key in the lock?

"Tessa?" he prodded in a gentle voice that didn't match his sharp gaze.

"I usually leave the key in that little nook beside the door. I don't remember leaving it in the keyhole."

"Okay." He nodded, took her arm and led her to the stairs. "Randal is on the porch. I want you to open the door and tell him what's going on. Don't go outside, though, okay?"

She hesitated. As much as she wanted Seth to take care of the problem, she knew that she shouldn't let him. Relying on other people usually led to heartache. She'd had enough of that to last a lifetime. "What are you going to do?"

"Check the attic, but I don't want you anywhere nearby when I do it."

"That's not necessary. I can just—"

"Do what I asked, okay, Tessa? It's the safest thing for both of us." He turned away, pulling gloves from his coat pocket and sliding them on.

"What if there *is* someone up there?"

"I can handle him. But not if you're in my way. Go tell Randal. It'll be good to have him around if I find someone."

"Okay. Fine," she mumbled, feeling like a coward as

she fled down the stairs. She heard the key turn in the lock and Seth's footsteps on the attic stairs.

"Where is Seth?" Logan asked as soon as she opened the door.

"The attic." She explained what she'd found, and Logan frowned.

"So, Seth went to check things out?"

"Yes."

"Great. Just what I need. A loose cannon," Logan responded with a sigh. "Go in the kitchen. Stay there until I give you the all-clear."

Logan was up the stairs before Tessa could move from her spot near the door.

A faint creak. The soft groan of old wood giving beneath heavy feet. She knew the sounds of the attic floorboards, could picture Seth and Logan moving through the cavernous room. All the boxes left behind by the people who'd come before her would make easy hiding places for anyone who might be lurking up there.

She shuddered, backing into the kitchen, her gaze on the ceiling, her muscles tense with fear and anticipation.

If they found someone, it would all be over. Bad guy caught and brought to jail—danger gone. Maybe the roses would stop, too. Maybe the past would finally fade into distant memories. She wanted that more than she'd wanted anything in a very long time. To let go. To breathe without the heaviness of secrets and fear pressing on her chest.

She wanted that, and sometimes she thought she could have it if she'd just allow God to give it to her. If she could just forgive Him for offering her everything and then taking it all away.

Tears filled her eyes, but she didn't let them fall. She hadn't cried since Daniel's funeral, and she wouldn't cry now. She'd trusted God, and He'd failed her. Not just with Daniel, with her parents, too. Twice, she'd lost everything. She wouldn't allow it to happen again.

Boots pounded on the stairs. The men were returning.

They walked into the kitchen, Logan slightly ahead of Seth, his eyes deeply shadowed, his smile kind. He looked like a guy who'd been through a lot, but who'd come out on top. The kind of person who could be counted on.

She didn't look at Seth. She knew what she'd see—confidence, strength, conviction. He could be counted on, too. He'd already proven that more than once, but she didn't want to count on him. Doing so could become a habit. One that she might find very difficult to break. "We didn't find anything, Tessa, but I'm going to dust the doorknob for fingerprints," Logan said.

"It could be that I forgot to put the key back the last time I went in the attic. My fingerprints might be the only ones you find." Now that they'd checked the attic and found it empty, she felt a little foolish. She wasn't one to overreact, and despite what she'd lived through in Kenya, she didn't jump at shadows.

"If they are, no problem, but I'd rather err on the side of caution than miss something. I'm going to get my fingerprint kit." Logan turned and walked out of the kitchen. Which left Tessa alone with Seth.

She couldn't avoid looking at him forever, so she met his eyes, was surprised by the sudden jolt of awareness that shot through her.

She'd been a widow for five years. In that time, she'd never even been tempted to go on a date. Friends had tried to hook her up with brothers or cousins or co-workers, and she'd always refused, because she hadn't wanted to feel the kind of longing that made a person vulnerable.

"I have to head out," he said, his gaze steady, his eyes deep blue. "You still have my card, right?"

"Yes."

"But, you're not planning to call even if your life depends on it?"

The comment made her smile. "If my life depends on it, I might call."

"How about we turn *might* to *will,* so I can get out of your hair and you can rest?" he responded, his Southern drawl more pronounced.

"I'm not sure I'm going to be able to rest," she admitted.

"Give it a try. You'll heal better if you do." He touched her cheek, his fingers brushing lightly down her jaw. Such a simple gesture, but longing shot through her, so intense that it filled her heart and her throat. "You're going to have a bruise there. You'd better put some ice on it."

She nodded, afraid if she spoke, he'd hear everything she was feeling. He frowned. "Maybe I should stick around until Randal gets back."

"I'll be fine." She forced the words out, because she really needed him to leave.

"You're sure?"

"Yes."

"Then, I'll see you next week."

"Wait!" she nearly shouted as he turned away.

He swung back around to face her again. "You changed your mind about wanting me to stay?"

"No, I..." What? She couldn't think of one good reason for calling him back. Except that she was scared and that as soon as left, she'd be alone again. "Just...thanks."

"Anytime." He walked down the hall, offering a brief smile as he stepped outside and closed the door. The house felt emptier without him in it, and that wasn't a good thing.

Tessa had been doing things on her own for so long, she'd forgotten what it felt like to have someone around. Seth made her remember.

After Logan finished dusting for prints, she'd face the attic head-on, drag her suitcase to her room and start packing, because she couldn't stay. Not just because of the danger that seemed to be dogging her, but because of Seth.

He was his own kind of danger.

The kind that could fill a woman's heart, seep into her soul. Make her want things that she shouldn't want. Long for things that were out of reach.

Tessa didn't want to go down that path again.

She didn't want the heartache it would bring.

Sometimes, though, she wanted more than a big old house and an oversize dog.

Sometimes, she wanted forever with someone she loved.

FIVE

"It's a little late for a phone call, isn't it?" Seth's older brother Grayson mumbled into the phone as Seth paced the living room of his small apartment.

He glanced at his watch.

"It's eleven o'clock," he responded.

Not such a bad time. Unless you lived on the East Coast like Grayson did.

"It's *two in the morning* here," Grayson growled, then mumbled something Seth couldn't hear.

"Sorry, bro. I always forget about the time difference."

"You still remember the cookie I stole from your lunch box when you were seven. There's no way you forgot the time difference."

Seth laughed and settled onto the sofa. "True."

"So, I guess you have a reason for waking me from a sound sleep?" Grayson's voice had already lost its edge, his normally good humor seeping into the words.

"You were the only one left on my list."

"What list?"

"The list of people I can call at any time of the day or night."

"So, what you're saying is that all of our siblings

have spouses and kids at home and you didn't want to wake them. Mom and Dad would go into cardiac arrest if the phone rang before dawn. But, since Honor and our kids are away for a week, you figured it would be okay to wake *me*," Grayson grumbled, but Seth knew his brother well enough to know that he was relieved to be getting the phone call. It had been a while since Seth had spoken to anyone in the family because he hadn't wanted to explain the extent of the reinjury to his shoulder. He also hadn't wanted to hear the lectures on doing too much too soon.

"Yeah, something like that."

"I'll keep that in mind the next time Honor wants to go help a friend through a difficult pregnancy." Grayson yawned and fabric rustled in the background. "So, what's the reason for this early morning phone call?"

"Does there have to be a reason? Maybe I just wanted to check in."

And maybe he'd also wanted to remind himself that he had family that he loved, a life that he loved. That things weren't quite as lonely and empty as the apartment had felt when he'd returned home to it.

"You mean the way that I wanted to check in a couple of dozen times this week during normal, decent hours?"

"You called me three times, Gray. That's not even close to a couple of dozen," Seth pointed out.

"And you didn't return my calls."

"I've been busy. Work. Therapy. You know the drill."

"How's the shoulder?"

"Better."

"Work?"

"Boring until I get off of desk duty."

"That only leaves your love life. So, who did you meet?" As per usual, Grayson cut right to the heart of the matter. A lawyer who worked in the small town where they'd grown up, he didn't believe in the fine art of small talk. Especially not when it took up time he could spend doing something else.

Like sleeping.

"I didn't meet anyone," Seth said, because Tessa didn't count as part of his love life, and he didn't need his entire family discussing the new woman in his life when he didn't actually have one. Although, he had to admit, a woman like Tess might tempt him to look for the things he'd had with Julia. Things he'd missed but hadn't thought he'd ever have again.

"Sure you didn't," his brother responded. "Who is she? Where did you meet? And how long before you introduce her to the family?"

"I guess being woken up at 2:00 a.m. has caused your ears to stop working," Seth retorted. "I said that I haven't met anyone."

"My ears might not be working, but my brain is. You haven't called anyone in the family for a couple of weeks, you didn't return any of my calls. Now, you're keen to get in touch. Woman trouble. That's the only explanation."

"Not trouble—"

"I knew it!" Grayson cut in. "Who is she?"

"*She* is my physical therapist, not my love interest, and she's in some serious trouble. I was at her place before I called you. I guess I just needed to hash the situation out, try to get a handle on what's going on so that I can help her."

"Are the police involved?" Grayson asked, all the amusement gone from his voice. No more joking or teasing. That was one of his best qualities—his ability to focus on a problem and work through it, to see the deep issues rather than the surface ones.

"Yes."

"Then maybe *you* don't need to be."

"I walked into the situation, Grayson. I'm not planning to walk out. Tessa needs someone besides the police on her side."

"And you want to be that person?" A simple question, but there was something in Grayson's tone that raised Seth's hackles.

"I told you, this isn't a love-interest kind of thing," he snapped.

"Right. Then what is it?"

Good question. One that Seth had absolutely no intention of trying to answer. "I called for some advice, Gray. How about you stop imagining things that aren't there and give me some?"

"Sure. I can do that. You talk while I make coffee. Maybe by the time you finish, I'll have a clear enough head to help."

Seth explained briefly, the wind howling against the window, rain splattering on the roof. Julia had never liked storms. She'd huddle in the corner of the sofa or hide beneath the covers, giggling nervously as thunder rumbled and the wind shrieked.

He frowned, his hand tightening on the phone.

"You still there, Seth?" Grayson's sharp question pulled Seth back from the past.

"Where else would I be?"

"In my reality, answering the question I just asked."

Seth would have been happy to answer if he'd heard it.

"What question?"

Grayson mumbled something under his breath, then

sighed. "I asked if your physical therapist actually wants your help, or if you just want to give it."

"I don't think Tessa wants anyone's help. Not even the police."

"Then maybe you should butt out."

"Like you butted out of Honor's life when she was in trouble?" Grayson had been anything but willing to turn away when his neighbor and her young daughter had needed his help. Now, they were happily married with two more children.

"And we've circled right back around to where we started. Woman trouble."

"It's too late at night to get into an argument—"

"So, now that my coffee is kicking in, you don't want to discuss things." Grayson chuckled. "I never pegged you for a coward."

"Let's stick to the facts, okay?"

"Fine, but you already know the facts. You know where to look if you're going to find Tessa's attacker— her past. You're going to have to start there."

He was right, of course. Seth *had* known that before he'd even called, but he and his siblings had always been close. When they had problems they turned to each other. That was the best part of family, and it was what he'd had with Julia. Until he'd failed her in the most basic of ways. "I can dig into Tessa's past all day long, Gray. That won't keep her safe."

There was a heartbeat of silence, and when Grayson spoke, the humor was gone again from his voice. "It's not your job to keep her safe, Seth. It's God's. If you want to help, great. But don't take the entire responsibility on your shoulders. That's way too heavy a burden to bear."

"I know. But I appreciate the reminder."

"Even though you're not going to listen to it?"

Probably not.

"How are Honor and the kids?"

"Changing the subject?"

"Yes."

"At least you're honest." Grayson laughed.

He spent the next fifteen minutes regaling Seth with tales of married life and parenthood. He made it sound chaotic, exhausting and pretty near perfect.

By the time Seth hung up, he was smiling. He was happy for Grayson. For all of his siblings. They'd found love, and they were making it last.

Seth had found it and lost it.

God's plan was always best. He knew that. Sometimes, though, knowing and believing weren't the same.

He climbed into bed fully clothed, closing his eyes and listening to the howling wind. He needed to sleep, but all that came were memories of the last time he'd seen Julia. Twenty-five and full of life, whispering in his ear that she'd be waiting when he got home.

His chest felt tight with the memory, and he threw his arm over his eyes, his shoulder protesting. He'd done too much, picking up Tessa's oversize dog and lugging him in and out of the house. Tessa wouldn't be happy when she saw him at his next appointment.

Not when. *If.*

Seth had a feeling she'd run if she had a chance. Leave town and try to outsmart whoever was following her.

His cell phone rang, and he grabbed it from his nightstand, his pulse jumping with anticipation. "Sinclair here."

"Seth?"

Tessa.

His heart jumped in acknowledgment, his hand tightening on the phone. "What's wrong?"

"Nothing. I just…"

"What is it, Tessa?" he prodded, keeping his tone light and easy. Tessa didn't seem like the type to panic over nothing, or to call someone at nearly midnight unless she *was* panicking.

"I just heard from Bentley's vet. She wants to keep him for a few days while the surgery site heals."

He doubted that was the reason she'd called, but he went with it. "How is he doing?"

"As well as can be expected. Amy did find a bullet in his haunch. It caused a hairline fracture in his hip. She thinks it will heal faster if she keeps him kenneled for a few days."

"She's probably right. Did she give the bullet to the police?" As he spoke, he got up, grabbed his handgun from the safe in his closet and shrugged into his side holster.

"Yes. So far, it's the only evidence Logan has. There weren't any usable fingerprints on the attic doorknob, and nothing in the woods," she said with a sigh. "I wonder if he'll find anything on the photo."

"It's possible," Seth said as he left his apartment. "Most criminals make mistakes, leaving evidence behind that they didn't mean to." He got in his truck and turned on the engine. The windshield wipers swiped at the frozen rain as he pulled away from the complex.

Something was bothering Tessa and it had nothing to do with evidence or her dog. He wanted to know what it was, and the quickest way to find out was to head over to her place.

"Is that why you called, Tessa? Because you're worried about the lack of evidence?"

"I... Yes. I'm sorry for calling so late about something so inane. I shouldn't have."

"I gave you my card so you could call if you needed me."

"I don't," she said quickly.

He wasn't sure why that bothered him, but it did. "Then, what *do* you need?"

Peace?

That's the answer Tessa wanted to give Seth, but how could she explain calling him in the middle of the night for something he couldn't give her? Something she couldn't even give herself?

"I need some information."

"About?"

Hiding. Leaving town and disappearing.

It sounded so silly now that she was about to say it. She rubbed her forehead, trying to ease her pounding headache. "I... This isn't really the time to discuss it. I really am sorry that I called you, Seth. I don't know what I was thinking."

"Stop apologizing, Tessa. It's annoying," he growled, but there was a touch of amusement in his voice, and she could almost see his smile. She wished she could tell him she needed *him* there, in her living room, telling her face-to-face that everything was going to be okay.

But *he* shouldn't be what she needed.

She pressed her forehead to the cold glass of the living room window, her eyes nearly watering from pain. Outside, ice pinged off the ground and stuck to tree branches. "I'll stop apologizing when you stop being so likable."

He laughed softly, the sound seeping through the phone and straight into a cold dark place in her heart. "What's wrong with being likable?"

"Nothing." She sighed. "Look, it's late, we're both tired…" Her words trailed off as headlights splashed across the road in front of her house, and a dark truck appeared. It slowed as it approached Tessa's place.

"Tessa?" Seth's voice sounded far away, fear making her lightheaded.

"Someone just pulled up outside my house," she whispered, as if whoever was in the truck could hear her through the glass and over the storm.

"That would be me."

"What?" She ran to the door, the phone still pressed to her ear as she opened it. "I told you that I didn't need you to come," she snapped into the phone.

"You told me that you didn't need *me,*" he replied. "That doesn't mean you don't need company."

She disconnected, watching as Seth got out of the truck and strode across the yard. He bounded up the porch stairs, the vibration of his feet on the wood seeming to echo through her aching head. She pressed her fingers to the bridge of her nose, but nothing would help the pain. Except for sleep, and she didn't think she'd ever be able to relax enough to get that.

"You're pale," Seth said without preamble, nudging her back inside.

"It's the lighting."

"Right. Come on. You need to sit down."

"Do you know how many times tonight you've told me to sit down?" she huffed.

"Obviously not enough, since you're still standing," he muttered, his hair dark from melting ice and rain, his chin scruffy from the beginning of a beard.

He looked good.

So good that she dropped onto the sofa just to put a little distance between them.

Her head throbbed and her stomach churned at the sudden motion, and she leaned back and closed her eyes.

"You okay?" Tessa felt Seth's fingers at the pulse point on her neck.

"Don't worry. My heart is still beating. I've just got a bad headache."

His fingers slipped from her neck to her shoulder, then fell away completely. The floor creaked, but Tessa was too afraid of losing what little she had in her stomach to open her eyes.

Minutes passed, the silence of the house settling around her. She was too exhausted to move, her head heavy and aching, her body numb from fatigue and grief and fear.

The floor creaked again, the cushion shifting as Seth sat beside her. "Here. This should help."

He pressed two tablets into her hand and dropped a cold cloth on the back of her neck.

"Thanks." She forced her eyes open.

He was so close she could see the small tracks of the stitches that had closed the wound at his hairline, and the faint white edge of the scar on his jaw. "How did you do it, Seth?" she asked.

"Do what?"

"Survive."

"What other choice was there?" He handed her a mug. "It's coffee. The caffeine will help the headache. I cooled it with a couple of ice cubes, so go ahead and take the medicine."

She did as he suggested, swallowing the pills down with a gulp of sweet lukewarm coffee. Her stomach lurched, then settled back into place.

"Good girl." He patted her arm, and heat zipped through her at the contact.

"I'm not a girl," she said, frowning into the coffee cup, more annoyed by her reaction to him than by his words.

"A figure of speech, Tessa, and a bad habit from dealing with my younger sister." He touched a strand of hair that had slipped from her ponytail. "I apologize. You are obviously a very capable, strong woman who just happened to need a cup of coffee and some pain reliever."

"And you're the buff hero who came to my rescue?"

He looked into her eyes for a long moment, studying her face. "No, I'm just the guy who happened to be at the right place at the right time."

"Thanks. For being here."

"Anytime." He stood and stretched, muscles rippling beneath his button-down shirt. "I'd better get home. It's late, and we both need to get some rest."

"I'll walk you out." She started to rise, but he put a hand on her shoulder.

"You're still pale. Stay here. Let the medicine kick in. I can find my own way out."

Seconds later, he was gone, the front door clicking softly, the freezing rain still falling against the roof.

She almost turned to look out the window, but she didn't want him to see her watching him leave. She didn't want him to think that she needed him to return because she didn't. After five years without Daniel, she'd gotten used to being alone.

Sometimes, though, being alone felt hollow and empty. Especially on nights when the wind was howling in the eaves and the blackness of the night pressed against the windows.

She shivered and dragged the old throw off the back of the couch, pulling it around her shoulders.

Sure, the storm was raging but storms didn't last forever.

Neither did troubles.

Not even the kind that seemed to be following her. Maybe she'd have to leave town. Maybe she'd have to start again somewhere else. If she did, she'd survive. Just the way she always had. It was what she did, what she'd always done.

Without help from anyone.

As long as she kept that in mind, she'd be just fine.

SIX

No more black roses or mysterious packages. Not a hint of danger, but five days after the attack, Tessa still felt hunted. Another day and Bentley would be home. With him around, she'd know danger was coming before it arrived. Until then, she'd continue to be hypervigilant—not that she had a choice. She didn't know how to throw the switch and turn off her nerves.

After a while, hyperawareness became...exhausting.

More than exhausting.

Tessa was bone-deep weary, her muscles aching from ten-hour days at Sam's office and countless hours pacing her house or running on her treadmill.

Trying to forget.

She hadn't been successful.

She pulled into her driveway, relieved to see lights shining from every window. She wasn't afraid of the dark, but she hated the way memories seemed to grow into sinister shadows when the lights were out and the house quiet.

She shrugged out of her coat as she stepped into the foyer and made her way to the kitchen where she tossed her purse onto the table and started the kettle. Not her normal routine. After work, she changed into her running gear and took Bentley out onto the trail. She'd done the same thing every night since she'd moved to town. Sun, rain, snow—the weather didn't matter. All that mattered was losing herself in the rhythm of the run.

She shoved her hands into the back pocket of her jeans, the fingers of her left hand brushing the business card Seth had given her.

She didn't know why she'd been carrying it.

Okay. She did know why. If she needed help, she knew she could ask him.

She just wasn't sure she *should* ask him.

She frowned and tossed the card into her junk drawer, poured boiling water over a tea bag and lifted the warm mug.

The phone rang, the sound so startling she sloshed hot tea onto her jeans.

"Ouch!" She muttered, swiping at the wet spot as she answered the phone. "Hello?"

"Tessa? It's Darius."

Tessa smiled at the sound of her friend's voice. "What's up?"

"I just thought I'd check in. Everything okay?"

"Yes, just like it has been every evening when you've checked in."

"I didn't call last night."

"Catherine did. We had a nice conversation about how overprotective you are," Tessa joked, but she didn't mind that Darius and his wife had been calling to make sure she was okay. As a matter of fact, it was nice to know that someone cared. She'd be giving that up if she left Pine Bluff. If she changed her name, went into hiding and started completely new, she'd be totally alone. No friends. No one to check in on her.

"If I were overprotective, I'd have someone staking out your house," Darius said wryly.

"No need for that. I'm tucked in snug as a bug in a rug. All the windows and doors locked and bolted."

"I'd be happier if you were tucked in with your be-hemoth of a dog."

"He'll be home tomorrow." And, hopefully, when he was, she'd finally get a little sleep.

"Glad to hear it. I'm actually calling because it's Wednesday-night potluck at church. Catherine and I were hoping you'd come."

"You've asked me to potluck every Wednesday since I moved to town, Darius. If I come, will you quit?" she asked with a sigh. It had been years since she'd attended church. She'd gone a few times after Daniel's death, but she'd always left feeling further from God than she'd ever thought she could be.

"If you come, I won't have to keep asking," he pointed out.

"Fine. I'll come. Give me the time and the address and—"

"Seven. We'll come pick you up."

"Afraid I'll change my mind?"

"Yes."

"I won't, but I'll drive myself." She wanted to make sure she could escape quickly if she felt the need. "There's a storm blowing in, and I don't want you to have to drive me back here if it hits before the potluck ends."

"It's only a twenty-minute drive."

"Twenty minutes is a long way when there's ice on the road. Now, how about you give me the address?"

Darius complied, and Tessa jotted the address on a piece of paper. She actually knew the church—she'd driven to it more than once, gotten as far as the parking lot and turned around.

"Got it," she said. "What should I bring?"

"Nothing. Catherine made her grandmother's famous BBQ meatballs, and there's enough for an army. See you there."

Tessa glanced at her watch. She had half an hour to kill before she needed to leave, but she didn't want to sit around waiting. Memories seemed to dwell in her solitude.

She grabbed her coat and walked outside, the cold wind biting through her coat and seeping into her bones. The meteorologists were calling for another ice storm, and thick clouds shrouded the moon and cast the evening in shades of white and gray.

In the distance, a coyote howled, the sound eerie and haunting. Other than that, the neighborhood was silent, Tessa's elderly neighbors tucked in for the evening.

Maybe she should be, too, but she was relieved to have something to do after five endless days of trying to forget that someone from her past wanted her dead.

She slid behind the wheel of her car and pulled out onto the empty road, following it to Pine Bluff Christian Church. The small white building stood in the foothills of the Cascade Mountains. Surrounded on all sides by thick pine forest, it seemed to glow in the darkness.

Tessa parked in the lot, positioning the car as close to the building as she could get it. Several people strolled toward the church, their laughter carrying on the cold night air.

Tessa didn't get out.

Instead, she leaned her head back, classical music drifting from the radio, the soft sounds of the congregation arriving mixing with it. She'd get out of the car eventually, but right at that moment, it felt good to imagine that there, in the parking lot of God's house, with dozens of people milling around, she was safe.

A sharp rap on the glass pulled her from half sleep and she opened her eyes, her heart tripping as she looked into Seth Sinclair's face.

"Didn't mean to startle you, Tessa," Seth said as Tessa opened her window. The last thing he'd wanted to do was scare her.

"What are you doing here?" she mumbled, her eyes cloudy with sleep. She looked tired, her skin a shade too pale, the bruises on her neck muted shades of blue and green.

"I attend church here." He reached in the window and flipped the door lock. "And it's potluck night." He held up a foil-covered casserole dish that he'd picked up at Catherine and Darius's place.

"You cook?"

"Does heating up soup from a can count?"

"No!" She laughed, closing the window and getting out of the car. "If you can't cook, where did you get the casserole?"

"It's meatballs. Catherine made them, but she can't make it tonight. Morning sickness in the evening, Darius said. He asked if I'd drop them off."

"Because he wanted you to check up on me?"

"Something like that." Seth didn't bother to deny it. He'd been working through the exercises Tessa had given him when the phone rang. Truth be told, he wasn't a potluck kind of guy. It just wasn't the kind of place a single guy hung out.

Unless he was looking for a single gal.

Which he wasn't.

"You don't seem like a potluck type of guy." Tessa echoed his thoughts, and he laughed.

"Truer words were never spoken. Maybe we should ditch this place and go get some real food," he suggested, surprising himself with the invitation.

Maybe he *had* come looking for a single gal—a very specific one.

One he hadn't been able to stop thinking about, no matter how many times he told himself he needed to.

Tessa hesitated, then shook her head. "It's probably best if we just do what we're supposed to."

"You sound like you're heading to the gallows." He took her arm and led her through the parking lot, automatically scanning the area for any sign of trouble. He didn't expect there to be any, but Darius had asked him to keep an eye on Tessa, and that's what he planned to do.

Of course, he would have done it, anyway, even if Darius hadn't asked him to.

"I don't mean to sound that way. It's just that going to church without Daniel seems strange."

"Daniel? Your husband?"

"Yes." Her cheeks heated. "That probably sounds silly. It's been five years—"

"You don't have to explain yourself, Tessa." He opened the door and she walked into the large vestibule ahead of him. "It took me nearly four years to feel comfortable going to family functions without my wife. After she died, I avoided them like the plague when I was home on leave."

"I didn't realize you'd been married."

"I was. Julia was killed by a drunk driver while I was in Afghanistan"

"I'm so sorry, Seth." She touched his wrist, her fingers barely brushing skin. Somehow, that was all it took. Heat raced up his arm, lodging somewhere in the vicinity of his heart, and suddenly all he saw was Tessa. Her deep-green eyes and fair skin, the freckles that dotted her nose and cheeks, the burnished red hair that curled against her neck.

Surprised, he took a step back. "Thanks," he managed to say. "Come on. Fellowship hall is this way."

He led her through the crowded hall and into a large room set up for the potluck. Dozens of tables filled the space, most of them already occupied by families or groups of friends.

He scanned the room, looking for an empty table.

"Seth! Over here!"

A small blond woman with a perky smile and bouncing curls nearly dislocated her arm trying to get Seth's attention. He wanted to ignore her, but he knew she'd persist. Peggy Sue Tanner was nothing if not determined.

"Peggy Sue." He offered the brief acknowledgment, hoping that would keep her away.

He should have known better. One of several women who considered Seth prime relationship real estate, she'd spent the past few months trying to convince him that they'd be a perfect pair.

"I thought you said you weren't coming tonight," she said as she hurried across the room. "If I'd known you were going to be here, I'd have saved a spot at our table."

"I had a last-minute change of plans. Right, Tessa?" He smiled at Tessa, hoping Peggy Sue would *finally* get the hint and decide to pursue someone else.

"Well," Peggy Sue murmured, a tiny frown line appearing between her brows as she gave Tessa a thorough once-over. "That worked out well, then, didn't it? Let's go find a table where we can all sit."

"We wouldn't want to tear you away from your friends, Peggy Sue." Tessa cut into the conversation, her arm sliding around Seth's waist. "Would we, Seth?"

"It's no problem. My friends will understand." Peggy Sue's frown line deepened.

"I'm sure they would, but we'll be fine on our own," Tessa replied, flashing the quick smile that showed off her dimple. "Seth, we'd better put these meatballs with the other food. It was nice meeting you, Peggy Sue."

She started walking, her arm still hooked around Seth's waist, her shoulder pressed to his side. She stayed there all the way to the food-laden tables that stretched across the back wall of the fellowship hall.

Seth couldn't say he minded.

Tessa felt *right*. It wasn't something that he could explain, but he didn't plan to question it, either.

He handed the dish to one of the women setting up the buffet, and did what he'd been thinking about from the moment Tessa's arm slid around his waist. He returned the gesture, his fingers curving against her warm side.

"I don't think she's watching any longer, Seth," she mumbled, tensing but not pulling away. "So, I guess I don't need to be glued to your side."

"Peggy Sue is persistent. It might be a good idea for us to stick together for a while longer," he responded, only half joking.

"How long is a while?"

"Just long enough to find a seat and get settled. There's a table in the corner." He led Tessa across the room, pulling out a chair for her.

She sat quickly, her cheeks tinged with pink, her gaze

lowered. She seemed embarrassed, maybe a little un-comfortable. Neither had been his intention.

He took the seat beside her, touching her wrist, ignor-ing the quick leap of his pulse. "I didn't mean to make you uncomfortable, Tessa."

"You didn't." She offered a half smile. "Much."

"I'd rather not have at all."

"I'm the one who started the whole thing. Remem-ber?"

He couldn't forget. Not the feel of her arm around his waist. Not the warmth of her fingers on his side. "I think we were both willing participants."

"Poor Peggy Sue," Tessa said, glancing over at the table where Peggy Sue sat with her friends. "She seems so…desperate."

"She's a nice lady. I'm sure she'll find someone."

"Just not you?" Tessa brushed a thick strand of hair from her cheek, her hand smooth, her fingers long and slender.

"No. Not me."

"You're not into dating?"

"I haven't been," he responded. Though he was be-ginning to think that the right woman might change his mind. "How about you?"

"No." She shifted uncomfortably.

"But you do eat, right?"

"Does snow fall in the mountains?" she replied.

He laughed, grabbing her hand and pulling her to her feet. "We'd better get in line, then. People around here know how to pack away food. We wait too long, and it'll all be gone."

He didn't release her hand, and she didn't pull away. Not when they walked across the room. Not when they were standing in the long line.

It felt…nice to be there with her, to listen to her talk about her day, about the clients she'd worked with and the satisfaction she'd felt when they progressed.

When they finally reached the table, she grabbed a plate and piled it so high she'd have given a hungry trucker a run for his money.

She must have noticed Seth eyeing her plate.

She snagged a dinner roll and tossed it on top of the pile of food. "What?"

"I'm just impressed that a woman your size can put away that much food."

"Obviously, you're easily impressed," she said with a smile.

He wasn't, but he decided not to tell her that. Why ruin their easy camaraderie?

They carried their plates back to the table, bowing their heads while the pastor blessed the food and the fellowship.

It was the same as any other potluck Seth had ever been to, but it felt different, the air lighter, the atmosphere warmer. Until Darius's phone call, he'd been planning to spend the evening at home. He was glad he'd let his mind be changed.

He would have told Tessa that, but she was picking at her food, looking about as comfortable as a cat in water.

"For someone who's hungry, you sure aren't eating much," he said.

She broke her dinner roll in half, slathered butter on it and set it back on her plate. "I have a lot on my mind."

"Want to tell me about it?"

"I'd rather you tell me about your day."

"You want to use my day as a distraction from your troubles?"

"Why not?"

"Because, desk duty isn't very distracting."

"Oh." She looked so disappointed, that he relented. "But, I might have a story or two that will work."

She smiled, stabbed at a bite of potato salad. "Let's hear them."

He wasn't big on talking about his work, but for Tessa, he'd make an exception.

He decided not to think too much about what that meant as he pushed aside his empty plate and began to speak.

SEVEN

Seth knew how to tell a story, and the stories he told about his job with Personal Securities Incorporated were designed to make Tess laugh.

They did. More than once.

But, even as she was laughing, she was thinking that she should leave.

Not because there were dozens of people around, eating and talking and having a great time while she picked at her food and tried to pretend that she wasn't enjoying Seth's company, but because all the pretending in the world couldn't change the way she felt when she looked in his eyes.

She swallowed a lump of potato salad and chewed another one as Seth finished explaining how he'd nearly been knocked out by an elderly woman when he'd walked into what was supposed to have been an empty dressing room at a ritzy bridal salon in Seattle.

"That did *not* happen!" she said on another breath of laughter.

"It did," he insisted. "She'd gone in there to nap while her granddaughter was fitted for a dress. After she attacked me with her purse, she accused me of trying to rush her to her grave. The whole time my client was trying on gowns, I was standing outside the door, being lectured by Mrs. Anderson."

She could picture him there if she let herself, all hard muscles and glittering blue eyes.

She put her fork down, her stomach churning with anxiety. She'd wanted something to take her mind off of her troubles. Seth was giving her a lot more than she'd bargained for. "Thanks for the distraction, Seth, but I'm more tired than I thought. I think I'd better get out of here."

"Running away won't change anything," Seth commented almost absently, his attention on a small group of people just entering fellowship hall. As relaxed as he seemed, he'd never stopped scanning the crowd or searching for signs of danger.

"Who says I'm running?" Tessa asked, frustrated with herself for being so transparent.

"Aren't you?" He turned the full force of his attention on her, his eyes dark and filled with things she didn't want to see. He had his own sorrow, his own pain. He didn't need to take on hers, and she didn't need him to do it.

"It's been a long few days. It's finally catching up to me," she responded, the half truth slipping out easily.

"Sure," he responded, dismissing her reason so definitively, her hackles went up.

"What's that supposed to mean?" she demanded.

"Just that I didn't take you for a chicken."

"I'm not!" she protested, pushing away from the table and standing. "I'm just tired."

"Okay." He eyed her dispassionately, not even a hint of humor in his face.

She thought she'd disappointed him.

She was sure she'd disappointed herself.

He was a good guy, a nice guy, and she was blowing him off.

She should say something, try to explain exactly why spending time with him was not a good idea, but Peggy Sue sauntered over, a brittle smile on her beautiful face.

"How are you two getting along over here?" she asked, stepping between Tessa and Seth.

It was as good an opportunity as any to do what Seth had accused her of.

She turned on her heels and hightailed it to the door.

Icy rain fell from the steel-gray sky, the moon hidden, the night silent but for the ping of precipitation hitting the ground.

Tessa picked her way across the parking lot, knowing without looking that Seth was behind her.

She could feel him as clearly as she felt ice sliding down her cheeks like cold tears. He grabbed her arm before she could open her car door.

Her heart jumped at the contact, her breath catching as she looked into his eyes.

"Next time, wait for me to check things out instead of running out half-cocked," he growled.

"I'm not one of your clients, Seth. You don't have to protect me."

"This isn't about me protecting you. It's about you making smart choices." His words were harsh but his hands were gentle as he took her car keys and unlocked the door. "Someone attacked you a few days ago and the police haven't found him yet. For all you know, he's lurking in the parking lot somewhere. Coming out here by yourself wasn't a good decision."

"You're right," she admitted, and he frowned.

"You made that a little too easy," he muttered.

"What?"

"I thought I was going to have to spend a lot of time convincing you that I should follow you home and make sure you got in safely."

"I may do things without thinking sometimes, but I usually don't repeat my mistakes." She snagged the keys from his hand and slid into the Mustang. "If you want to escort me home, I'm not going to argue." She closed the door, cutting off the conversation. Her heart beat a strange uneven rhythm, her pulse sloshing in her ears. She wanted to think it was from fear, but she knew better. She'd fallen hard when she'd met Daniel.

She couldn't fall again.

Seth walked to his truck and climbed into the cab, Headlights splashed across the parking lot, and he waved for her to precede him.

She pulled out onto the road, moisture drying on her cheeks. It felt like all the tears she'd wanted to cry but hadn't. Days' worth. *Years'* worth.

She shuddered.

Seth could follow her home.

He could walk her to her door.

But he could never be anything other than what he was, because if she let him, she'd have to risk it all again. Her hopes. Her dreams. Her heart.

She wasn't willing to do that. It hurt too much to lose everything.

But it hurt a lot not to have everything, too.

It hurt to live in an empty house when she'd always wanted children to fill it. It hurt to go to church alone, to spend Christmas alone. To wake up on her birthday and know there was no one to celebrate with.

She swallowed back tears, frustrated with her melancholy mood, irritated because she'd come to terms with her life and she loved it just the way it was. She didn't *need* anyone to fill the lonely place in her heart.

Still…it would be nice.

Ice pinged off the windshield and bounced off the road. As winter storms went, this one wasn't bad, but Tessa's nerves were already shot, her palms sweaty as she navigated the winding country road that led to her house.

It seemed to take forever, but she finally pulled into her driveway, put the Mustang in park and wiped her sweaty palms on her jeans.

The porch light was off. So was the living room light. No lights shone from the upstairs windows. None from the foyer.

She hadn't left the house that way.

She glanced up and down the street. Her neighbors were a good distance up the road, but their lights shone through the darkness. The streetlights glowed hazy yellow in the storm.

Everyone but Tessa seemed to have electricity.

Maybe it wasn't the electricity at all. Maybe someone had turned off the lights. Maybe that same someone was waiting in the darkness.

Someone tapped on her window, and she screamed, the sound dying abruptly as she met Seth's eyes.

She opened the door, her heart slamming against her ribs. "What are you doing out there!"

"I followed you home, remember?" he asked, frowning as he studied her face. "What's wrong?"

"The lights in the house are off. I left them on."

"You're sure?" He glanced at the house, shifting so that his body was between her and it.

"Yes. Maybe the electricity went out. Sometimes—"

"The streetlight in front of your house is on. I don't

think it's an electricity problem. Call the police. I'm going to check things out."

"No!" She grabbed his hand. "Let the police handle it."

"If someone is in there, Tessa, I'm not willing to give him a chance to slip out the back door and get away." He gave her hand a gentle squeeze. "Give me the house key."

"Seth, I really don't think this is a good idea."

"But, you thought that walking out of the church alone was?"

"No, but that was different. I—"

"Was alone and without protection. I'm carrying a concealed firearm. Come on, Tess. This is what I do for a living. Stop wasting time, and give me the key." He held out his hand, and she dropped the key into it, not sure what else to do.

If someone was waiting in the house, it *was* better to find him and catch him than let him escape.

But, she felt like a coward letting Seth walk into danger while she waited in the car.

"Stay in the car and lock the doors."

"Seth—"

"I mean it, Tessa. Call the police and stay here." He slammed the door, and she dialed 911, watching as he disappeared into the dark house. The operator asked questions and Tessa answered, but her mind wasn't on the conversation. It was on Seth.

Ice fell from the deep-gray sky, coating the driveway and grass, and hanging from the old cedar that stood at the edge of Tessa's yard. Aside from the quiet ping on the roof of the car, the world lay hushed and still. She expected at any moment to hear a gunshot, to see a flash of light in the darkness of her house.

Time ticked by, and she saw nothing, heard nothing but the muted sounds of approaching police cars.

Please, Lord, keep him safe.

The prayer flitted through her mind, and she held on to it, tried to believe that this time, her prayers would be answered. Such a hard thing to believe when her most heartfelt prayer had been ignored.

She frowned.

Not ignored. Just not answered the way she'd wanted, expected, needed.

Please, Lord.

She tried again, shifting in her seat and staring at the empty road, willing the police to arrive and willing Seth to be okay until they did.

Seth eased through the living room and into the dining room, following the track of smudged footprints on the wood floor. He held his Glock in hand and ready, his nerves humming with adrenaline. The house was silent, but something felt off. He just couldn't put his finger on what it was. He searched the dark corners of the dining area and walked into the kitchen.

Nothing there, but he felt danger the same way he had countless times when he'd worked in enemy territory.

He crouched low, making himself a smaller target as he eased across the empty kitchen and approached the mudroom. Cold air swept in on a gust of wind that splattered ice onto the mudroom's tile floor.

Surprised, Seth straightened, walking into the small room, his feet sliding across the soaked tiles.

The door to the backyard stood open, the deck beyond completely coated with ice. Whoever had opened the door had done it a while ago. No footprints showed in the ice.

Seth crouched, studying the area more carefully, his shoulder throbbing from the cold, his mind calculating the time it would have taken for a footprint to be completely covered.

The sound of sirens reached a crescendo as Seth walked into the yard and tried to find footprints in the icy grass.

Nothing.

Again.

Frustrated, he holstered his gun and walked back into the house as the front door opened and a police officer called out.

Backup had arrived.

But whoever had been in the house was already gone.

"Back here," he called out, turning on the light and letting it fill the old-fashioned kitchen. Tessa had left the place spotless. Not a pan or a pot in sight. Not a smudge on the granite counters. Footsteps pounded in the hallway, and Logan walked into the kitchen.

"Why am I not surprised to see you here, Sinclair?" he grumbled as he crossed the room.

"I wasn't going to let the guy escape if he was in here."

"So Tessa said," Logan responded, glancing around the kitchen. "I would have preferred you not contaminate the crime scene."

"I didn't touch anything without gloves."

"You trampled any evidence the guy might have left on the floor." Logan crouched, studying Seth's footprints and the floor around them.

"Aside from a few smudges on the floor in the foyer and living room, there aren't any prints. The back deck is clear, too," Seth offered.

"That's not the point, Seth, and you know it." Logan

straightened. "Next time, I want you to wait for law enforcement."

"I'll keep that in mind," Seth responded dryly. He'd done what he'd thought he had to, and he'd do it again if it meant catching the guy who was after Tessa. "I think he came in the front door and left out the back."

"Any reason for that?"

"The front door was unlocked when I got here. Tessa isn't the kind of person to leave the house without securing it."

"I'll ask her."

"Ask me what?" Tessa walked into the room, her skin leached of color, her hair wet from melting ice.

"You're supposed to be waiting in your car, Tessa." Logan ran a hand down his jaw and shook, obviously as frustrated as Seth felt.

"It was freezing outside." She turned her attention to Seth, her eyes the same deep green of the mountains in the spring. "Are you okay?"

"I'd be better if you hadn't disobeyed orders."

"I thought we already discussed the whole taking orders thing. I don't do it well."

"You'd better learn to, because whoever is after you isn't playing games," he snapped, irritated with her stubbornness. If she wasn't careful, it would get her killed.

"I'm not the one who walked into a dark house alone when anyone could have been hiding in it, remember?" she responded with a scowl.

"I remember that I told you to stay in the car."

"Neither of you should have come in here," Logan cut in. "At the rate we're going, we'll have contaminated every stick of evidence there is. Go back out to Tessa's car. Both of you. Wait there until I call you back in."

Private security wasn't the same as law enforcement,

and once the police arrived, Seth usually backed off and let them take over. But he was tempted to do things differently this time. He wanted to search every corner of the house himself, just to be absolutely sure that nothing was missed.

He also wanted to make sure that Tessa stayed safe. Her attacker wasn't in the house. That meant he was somewhere else. That could mean miles away or inches.

"Come on," he took her hand, tugging her out of the kitchen. He touched his free hand to his Glock as they stepped outside, searching the darkness. Ice still poured from the sky, but there was a gentleness to it, a quietness that belied any danger.

Tessa slid into her Mustang and he closed her door, then went around to the other side, his shoulder throbbing from cold and tension.

By the time he got in the car, Tessa had the engine running and the heater pouring hot air out of the vents.

She eyed him as he settled into the seat, her gaze touching his face, his shoulder, the gun that peeked from beneath his coat.

"Your shoulder hurts," she said.

"Not much."

"Right." She scooted onto her knees, leaning across the space between them, her hair brushing his chin as she prodded the offending joint.

"Hey!" He pulled back as she found the sorest spot. "My appointment isn't until tomorrow."

"You need to ice that tonight, Seth. You've got some inflammation in the joint. If you're not careful—"

"Tessa." He grabbed her hand as she tried to touch his shoulder again. "I have a doctor. I don't want another one."

"Sorry." She smiled sheepishly. "I guess I'm just trying to keep my mind off of whatever is going on in the house."

"I can think of a few other ways to do that,"

"Like what?" she whispered, her gaze dropping to his lips.

Without thinking, he slid a hand up her arm and under the heavy fall of her hair. Her skin was cool and velvety, her hair silky. It wouldn't take much to close the distance between them. Not much at all.

Not the right time, though. Not the right place. "I could tell you a few more stories about Mrs. Anderson."

"The old lady who attacked you with her handbag?" she said with a shaky laugh.

"That would be the one."

"You saw her again?" She settled into her seat, her hand still in his. She didn't try to pull away, and he didn't let her go. He liked the connection, the warmth of her palm, the way it seemed to fit so perfectly in his.

"She sends me a Christmas card every year."

"No way!"

"She says she wants to keep track of me. Make sure I'm not peeking in on any other unsuspecting women."

Tessa laughed, and he wondered what it would be like to taste the sound on her lips.

Her laughter died, her eyes wide and wary.

"Tess," he began, but the front door of the house opened, light spilling out onto the porch.

"Logan is finished," she said, jumping out of the car before he could continue.

It was probably for the best.

He wasn't sure what he would have said.

God had brought him into Tessa's life for a reason, but aside from keeping her safe, Seth hadn't figured out what that might be.

Not that he didn't have some ideas.

As a matter of fact, he had several very interesting ones.

He shoved the thought away and got out of the car, cold air cooling his heated skin as he followed Tess across the yard.

EIGHT

Tessa ran up the porch stairs and skidded to a stop a foot from Logan, her heart pounding frantically. Thank goodness he'd opened the front door before she'd made a complete and utter fool of herself.

She'd come within seconds of kissing Seth.

And with Seth, one kiss would never be enough. She'd want more. More kisses, more time, more attention.

More him.

More of all the things that made a couple…a couple.

Only she and Seth were *not* a couple.

They were just two people whose lives had collided.

"We're not in a huge rush, Tessa," Logan said dryly. "There's no reason to run."

"I was just anxious to see if you found anything. Did you?" she asked, her pulse thudding in her ears as Seth walked up behind her.

She could feel him there, like warm sunlight on a winter day, and she had to force herself not to turn around and look into his face. She knew what she'd see. The same thing she was feeling—confusion, excitement, maybe even a little fear.

"I thought I'd let you tell me." Logan's gaze shifted

from Tessa to Seth and back again. Did he sense the tension that still shimmered in the air?

It didn't matter. What mattered was finding the person who'd been in her house. Tessa shut out everything else. Seth. Her frantically racing pulse. "What does that mean?"

"There's something…strange in your bedroom."

Her stomach churned and her mouth went dry. "It's not alive, is it?"

"No. How about we go up and take a look?"

"I'd rather you just tell me what it is," she mumbled, but neither man seemed to hear. They were both already heading up the stairs, the old wood creaking beneath their feet.

The last thing she wanted to do was follow them.

Unfortunately, she didn't think she had a choice.

Her feet felt mired in cement, every step more difficult than the last. She paused at the landing, eying the door to her bedroom.

Logan motioned for her to continue. "Come take a look. Just don't touch anything."

That would be hard to do seeing as how her feet were permanently attached to the top stair.

"It's going to be fine," Seth said, grabbing her hand and dragging her the last few feet to the bedroom door.

Dozens of black rose petals covered her bed and trailed onto the floor around it. In the middle lay a large copy of the photo that had been in the envelope. She stepped forward, the sickeningly sweet scent of roses hanging in the air.

Her stomach heaved, and she leaned forward, hands on her knees, eyes closed, a dozen images flashing through her head. Daniel. Andrew. Blood. Fire.

"Take a deep breath, Tess," Seth murmured, his

breath tickling the hair near her ear, his palm cool and dry against her neck.

"I take it you didn't leave the room like this?" Logan asked.

"What kind of stupid question is that, Randal?" Seth snapped, his hand sliding from Tessa's neck to her back.

She straightened, her heart skipping a beat as she looked at the bed, the flowers, the photograph. "Why would I?"

"I don't know, but I had to ask. I'm not doing my job if I don't check every angle," Logan responded, snapping a photograph of the bed and a close-up of the picture. He lifted it in gloved hands, studying the image for a long moment. "This is a copy of the picture you received with the tarantula."

It wasn't question, but she answered, anyway. "That's right."

"It was taken in Kenya?"

"Yes." The picture had been taken a month after they'd moved there. She'd answered the same questions the night she'd been attacked. She knew Logan remembered. She didn't want to talk about it all again. Didn't want to rehash all the old memories, all the old dreams. She wanted to tell him that, but her heart thrummed like a hummingbird's wings, her breath catching in her throat.

Seth touched her cheek. "Take a deep breath, Tess."

"I'm okay."

"Then why do you look like you're going to pass out?" he muttered.

Probably because she *felt* like she was going to pass out.

Before, she could say that, she was in Seth's arms, and he was carrying her from the room.

"Put me down before you hurt your shoulder," she protested.

He ignored her, carrying her down the stairs to the old rocking chair. He set her there, pulling the throw from the couch and wrapping it around her shoulders.

"Better?" he asked, cupping her face with both hands and studying her intently.

"I wasn't going to pass out," she said.

"Sure you weren't."

"I *wasn't*. And, even if I *was,* you shouldn't have carried me down here. You're going to be a mess when you come in for therapy tomorrow."

"I don't think you should go to work tomorrow, Tess," he said, his hands sliding away. "As a matter of fact, I don't think that you staying here tonight is a good idea."

"I've been staying here every night since I was attacked. Nothing has happened."

"Nothing has happened until now." Seth walked to the window, fingered the old lock. "Do you know how easy it would be for someone to break the lock on this window?"

"No, but—"

"You don't have an alarm system, your backyard opens to woods, your closest neighbor is a quarter mile away. For all we know, our perp is waiting for everyone to leave before he strikes again."

"He's making some good points," Logan said as he walked into the room. "I'm going to assign a patrol car to your street, but do you have a friend you could stay with for the night?"

Darius and Catherine would be happy to offer her a place to stay, but Catherine was five months pregnant, and there was no way Tessa was going to put her in the line of fire. She didn't want to drag *any* of her friends into danger.

So, maybe this was it.

Maybe the time to pack her bags and move on had finally come.

"I can leave town for a while," she said, and both men frowned.

"And go where?" Logan asked.

"I…don't know, but anywhere is better than here, right?"

"If that's the way you feel, then I can arrange a place," Seth broke in. "Just give me a few minutes to make some phone calls."

"I can handle it myself," she tried to protest, but he was already in the foyer and walking out the door.

No way did Seth think that leaving town was the answer to Tessa's problems. If she ran, her troubles would find her.

He expected her to follow him outside, insist that she could take care of herself.

She didn't, and he stood on the porch, scanning the dark street as he called his boss. It only took a few minutes for Seth to get permission to use the company's safe house.

By the time he returned to the living room, color had returned to Tessa's face, and she looked a lot less fragile.

"We're set," he told her, bracing himself for what he knew was coming.

"Set for what?"

"I have a place for you to stay."

"What place?"

"We can discuss that on the way."

"I'd rather discuss it now." She stood, swaying a little. The bruises on her neck were fading, but the circles under her eyes were deep.

"What we really need to discuss," Randal broke in, looking up from a small notebook he'd been writing in, "is a list of people who were on the mission trip to Kenya with you and who were affiliated with it."

"The organization who sponsored us would have that. Only a few people survived the massacre." Tessa rattled off the name of the group she'd traveled with. There was no emotion in her voice, no hint of what she was feeling.

"I'll give them a call, see if anyone else is having the kind of trouble you are."

"If they are, I haven't heard anything about it."

"You keep in touch?"

"No. Not in the last few years, anyway."

"Then, it's something I'll need to check on. If there's anything else you can tell me—"

"There isn't," she said too quickly.

"That was an awfully quick response," Seth pointed out.

She shrugged, her hair sliding across her shoulders, silky red against her dark coat. "Because there isn't."

"I can't help you if you're not upfront with me," Logan said, his gaze sharp and hard.

"I'm being as upfront as I can be."

"I'm not sure that's the same as being as upfront as you *should* be," Logan pointed out. "Tell you what. Why don't you sleep on it? Decide whether keeping your secrets is worth losing your life?"

"I—"

"Call me once you get her settled in, Seth." Logan cut off her protest. He stalked from the room, the stairs creaking as he retreated.

"Come on." Seth took Tessa's arm, as frustrated as Logan seemed to be.

She was hiding something.

It was obvious, but she seemed determined to keep her secret. No matter what it cost.

They walked outside, her muscles tense and tight. She didn't speak as he helped her into the truck. Didn't ask where they were headed or why he thought it was his right to take her anywhere.

He pulled away from the house, checking his review mirror, looking for any sign that they were being watched.

Nothing. Not even a shadow moving in the breeze.

"You're quiet," he finally said.

"I don't have much to say."

"I think you mean that you don't have much you're *willing* to say," he responded. Unlike Logan, he wasn't ready to let things go.

"Maybe you're right. And, maybe Logan is right, too, but I've been...quiet for a long time, and I don't know if I can say what I need to without hurting a lot of people."

"So you'll let yourself be hurt, instead?"

She didn't respond, and he glanced her way as he merged onto the interstate.

She was staring out the window as if the answers she needed were somewhere out in the darkness. He could have told her that they weren't, but he touched her knee instead, letting his hand rest there for just a moment before he pulled it away. "Tess, whatever you're hiding, it's going to come out eventually."

"I hope not," she whispered so quietly he barely heard the words.

He let them lie, let the truck fall silent again, because

her voice had been tinged with tears, and he didn't think making her cry was going to accomplish his goal.

Whatever secrets she had, she was holding them close. Whether she wanted them to or not, eventually, they'd be revealed. It was the only way to keep her safe, the only way to keep her from being consumed by whatever she was running from.

NINE

The roads were horrible, the ice slick and shiny on the black pavement. It was so much easier for Tessa to focus on that than on the silent truck and her silent companion.

She didn't want to discuss her past, because there were too many pieces of if that she couldn't reveal, but she didn't have a death wish, either. Getting a rose once a year was one thing, being attacked, having her house broken into and her dog shot—those were other things entirely.

Logan had been right. She needed to think things over, decide how much she was willing to sacrifice for the legacy that had been built out of the ashes of the massacre.

She rubbed her forehead, willing away the headache that was throbbing behind her eyes.

"You're tense," Seth said, kneading the muscles at the base of her neck, his fingers firm and warm and so nice that she wanted to relax against him.

"That happens when someone breaks into my house and leaves black rose pedals all over my bed."

"It's nothing to joke about, Tess."

"I'm not joking."

"Good, because if I hadn't been with you when you'd

returned to the house…" His voice trailed off, and he left the rest to her imagination.

Not a good thing, because she had a great imagination. One that filled in all the words he hadn't said. "Thanks for following me home. You probably saved my life."

"You can thank me by telling me about your trip to Kenya."

She hesitated.

She hated talking about Kenya. Hated that everything she'd believed in when she'd lived there had died with Daniel. "It was my husband's dream. He wanted to go and build orphanages and schools and dig wells."

"His dream and not yours?" He asked the question she'd been asking herself for years. One she had never quite found an answer to.

"Sometimes I think that. Other times, I know that I was just as excited and enthusiastic as he was. We left for Africa the year after I graduated from college. Daniel thought we'd probably spend the rest of our lives there. He did. I came home alone."

"I'm sorry, Tessa." Seth took her hand, his thumb caressing her wrist, the warmth of it chasing away the chill that filled her every time she thought about Daniel's enthusiasm, his passion, his zeal for Kenya. Hers had been a pale reflection of his, a tiny shimmer compared to the bright light that had consumed him.

"Me, too. I think this is the way Daniel would have wanted it, though. I think he's probably happy that he died doing what God called him to."

"You sound bitter."

Did she?

Maybe she was. "I never minded being second to God. That's the way it should be. But…" She stopped, because saying what she was thinking felt too much like a betrayal.

"You would have liked to have been first after Him?"

"Daniel was a good husband." She jumped to his defense. He *had* been a good husband, but he'd been a better missionary.

"I don't think that I said he wasn't," Seth said quietly. "If you thought that's what I was implying, I apologize."

"Are you always so agreeable, Seth?"

"I'd like to say that I am, but I think my family would probably disagree."

"You have a big family?" she asked, more than happy to change the subject.

"Three brothers and a sister. Assorted nieces and nephews. My folks."

"You're close?"

"Sometimes too close. As a matter of fact, they hovered so much after I shipped back from Afghanistan, I had to move across the country to get some breathing room."

"I don't believe that."

"It's true. I didn't want them wasting their time worrying about me when they all have families to take care of." The fondness in his tone was unmistakable, and Tess wondered what it would be like to have that kind of relationship. From the time she was little, family was all that she'd wanted. She'd been smart enough to know that it wasn't what she had with her parents. Married young and still partying hard, they'd had little time for their only child. When they died in a car accident, she'd been left alone. She hadn't felt any lonelier after their deaths than she had been when they were alive.

"How about *your* family," Seth asked a he exited the freeway. "Are they around?"

"My parents died when I was a kid. I don't have siblings."

"Grandparents?"

"No. I grew up in foster care and spent most of my teenage years being shipped from one placement to another."

"That must make for lonely holidays."

"I have friends. And Bentley." Her life sounded… pitiful, but it wasn't, and she wanted Seth to know that. "I'm happy with my life. I like it just the way it is."

"Good to know," he responded easily.

She pressed her lips together to keep from expanding on the joys of being alone.

The truth was, she *did* enjoy her life, but she wouldn't have minded having a family to spend time with.

"Did you grow up in Pine Bluff?" he asked, and she wasn't sure if simple curiosity led to the question or if he was trying to figure out the secrets he'd insisted she was keeping.

Secrets she *was* keeping.

"No. I'd never even heard of it before I attended Darius's wedding. It's such a nice area, I decided it would be a good place to settle down."

"Because you thought you could hide here?"

"It wasn't really about hiding. It was more about…"

"Not getting a rose on the anniversary of your husband's death?"

"Yes."

"Contacting the authorities might have been a better way to go."

"Until recently, I didn't think I was in danger."

"A black rose isn't a token of love, Tessa," he pointed out, and she knew he wanted an explanation. Some reason as to why she hadn't been afraid for her safety.

She couldn't tell him. Not without revealing everything. "I thought it was just a...reminder."

"Who would think that you needed one?"

They were heading into dangerous territory again. She could tell from the sudden tension in the air that Seth knew it. As a matter of fact, she was pretty sure this was exactly where he'd been leading their conversation since it began. "I'm not sure."

"But, you have an idea, right?" He turned onto a street near Spokane's Riverfront Square, old buildings butting up against new ones, all of them brightly lit and beautiful.

"The fact that you're withholding the truth isn't helping either of us," Seth continued when she didn't speak.

"I'm sorry."

"Sorry isn't going to help if you die." He drove into a parking garage, driving up to the nearly empty top floor and parking near the building entrance.

"Seth..." She didn't know what she wanted to say, wasn't sure what she *could* say.

He touched her shoulder. "Unless you're going to tell me everything I want to know, don't bother, okay?" The words were gentle, but his gaze was implacable.

She could feel the heat of his fingers through the thick layers of her coat and shirt. For some reason, that made her eyes burn and her throat clog.

When she didn't speak, his hand dropped away. "The safe house is inside this building. Don't get out of the truck until I come around to your side."

"Safe house?"

"The company I work for owns it. We use it for clients who aren't safe in their homes and communities."

"I'm not a client."

"No, but you're a friend, and that counts for a lot."

He got out of the truck and shut the door, sealing her in with her thoughts and her silence.

He was probably angry, and she didn't blame him. He and Logan were doing everything they could to keep her safe and to find her attacker. She was thanking them by keeping secrets.

She didn't want to.

She really didn't, but she wasn't sure what else to do. In the years since the massacre, she'd prayed for direction and she'd asked for guidance. All she'd found was emptiness and fear.

Please, God, just help me know what to do.

She tried again, the words spinning through her mind and flying out into the universe. She wanted so badly to believe that God heard them. She wanted so much to grab hold of the faith that she'd had the year she'd traveled to Kenya.

Seth opened the door, the scars on his face faded evidence of all that he'd been through. He hadn't let physical scars become emotional ones, though. He hadn't let trials steal his faith or his joy.

"Ready?" He offered a hand, and she took it, his rough palm pressed against hers, the warmth of it more comforting than anything had been in a very long time.

"Yes," she responded.

He led her through the parking garage and into an old elevator. It clanked closed, sealing them in.

Tessa had never been claustrophobic but the walls seemed too close. Seth seemed too close, that wintery fresh scent that always seemed to cling to him drifting in the air, bringing back memories of things she'd tried hard to forget.

Like the way it felt to stand in the shelter of someone's arms. After Daniel's death, she'd craved that. She'd longed to be close to someone again. To hug and be hugged. To link fingers and press palms close.

The elevator door slid open and she nearly jumped out, her heart hammering frantically.

"Slow down, Tessa. You'll be safe once we're in the apartment. Until then, stick close." Seth snagged the back of her coat, pulling her up short.

"Where is the apartment?" She avoided his gaze, afraid he'd see the longing in her eyes.

"Upstairs."

His left hand slid around her waist as he led her to a door at the far end of the hall. A security system panel on the wall was padlocked. Seth pulled a key from his pocket and unlocked it, then entered a code into the keypad beneath, his left hand still curved around her waist.

She didn't pull away. She didn't want to, and that terrified her almost as much as everything else.

Seth opened the door into a small entrance hall. Narrow stairs led up to another door and another panel. He hadn't been kidding when he'd said she'd be safe there.

She glanced over her shoulder, sure that she'd see someone barreling through the door they'd just come in.

"Relax," Seth murmured. "We've got security cameras inside and outside the building. If anyone followed us, Taryn would have already called me."

"Taryn?"

"The other security specialist that will be working with me tonight. She's not on a case so she volunteered to come out and lend a hand."

"On a night like this?"

"She's an interesting person. Her priorities are a little different than most, and she loves a challenge." He punched his password into the security panel and opened the door.

The apartment beyond was spacious and pristine— dark hardwood floors, streamlined and modern furniture. The oversize living room opened into a dining area and an upgraded kitchen. The place looked lived in and well cared for. Nothing like what Tessa imagined a safe house would look like.

Not that she'd spent much time imagining one.

"That you, Sinclair?" a woman called from a hallway to the right of the living room.

"Who else would it be?" Seth responded, moving into the kitchen.

Tessa followed, watching uncomfortably as he bent over a computer monitor set up on the counter.

She should have insisted on leaving town. That would have felt a lot less awkward than standing in a small room with the man who made her heart flutter and her pulse race.

Just then, a petite blonde walked down the hall, her hair pulled into a slick chignon, her makeup perfect. She wore a long black dress, four-inch heels and drop earrings that looked like real diamonds. She could have been a model or a high-fashion socialite if not for the gun holster strapped low on her hip.

"Interesting look, Taryn." Seth barely looked up from the computer, but Tessa couldn't *stop* looking.

"I was on a date, pal, and I haven't had a chance to change." She walked into the kitchen and offered Tessa a hand. "I'm Taryn, and you must be Tessa."

"That's right."

"Hear you're having a little bit of trouble." She leaned against the doorjamb, her cornflower-blue eyes showing just a hint of amusement.

"I am, but I wish Seth hadn't dragged you away from your date."

"He didn't. Our boss did. And I was thrilled to get the phone call. The guy I was out with was about as boring as an afternoon in front of the television." Taryn grinned. "Come on. I'll show you your room while Seth stares at the monitor."

"Someone has to stare at it, Tar." Seth finally looked up, and Tessa's breath caught, her heart shimmying.

His hair was just a little long, his eyelashes thick and golden. The scars on his face gave him a look of implacable toughness, but his eyes were the deep blue of the summer sky.

How had she ever thought he was average?

"Nothing has moved on that street in forty minutes. Too much ice," Taryn said. "But if you want to waste your time, feel free. Come on, Tessa. Your room is at the end of the hall. I'll go over the rules on the way."

"Rules?" Tessa tore her gaze from Seth.

"Did you think you'd get to stay here without them?" Taryn pulled Tessa from the kitchen. "No cell phone while you're here. As a matter of fact, let me see it."

She held out her hand. Tessa dug the phone from her purse, handed it over and watched as Taryn took out the battery and then handed the phone back to her.

"Hey—"

"You can have it back when you leave."

"I'm not going to—"

"We all have good intentions, Tess, but temptation can get the best of anyone. There's no internet access in here, but there is a television." She pushed open a door at the end of the call and gestured for Tessa to walk in ahead of her.

"I thought you said watching TV was boring," Tessa protested as she stepped into an oversize room.

"It's better than watching the wall." Taryn grinned.

"The bathroom is through that door. It's stocked. You'll find clothes in the dresser and closet. You're tiny, but I think there's probably something that will fit you."

"I'm not—"

"If you need anything, give us a holler. Seth will probably stay glued to the screen until his shift is over, but I can get you what you need. First, though, I have *got* to get out of this dress." She plucked at the silky fabric. "A waste of time shimmying into it, I'll tell you that. See you in a bit."

She walked into the hall and shut the door, leaving Tessa alone. Tess glanced around the room. Everything she needed was there. Bed. Dresser. Closet. A couple of chairs. And, of course, a television. All she needed was Bentley and she could hunker down until the trouble passed.

She frowned, not happy with the thought.

She'd been running for years, but that didn't mean she'd expected others to step in and take care of her problems. She was perfectly capable of doing that herself. So, why was she standing in a room while Seth manned a security monitor?

Maybe, because she was too afraid to face him again, too afraid that what she felt when she was near him wasn't just a product of fatigue or fear. She dropped onto the bed. Her head throbbed with every heartbeat, but she didn't have the energy to go look for medication.

Voices and quiet laughter drifted into the room.

Seth and Taryn.

They'd be the perfect couple, both of them good looking, confident and accomplished.

She lay back on the bed, listening for several more minutes. She could go out and join them, but it was better this way. The two of them doing what they did best while she...

Hid?

She didn't like how that made her feel, but it was the truth. She *was* hiding. Not just from her past. From Seth. And, she was just enough of a chicken to let herself do it.

She sighed, pulling the pillow over her head and pressing it against her ears as she tried to will herself to sleep.

TEN

Seth stared at the computer while Taryn gave him every minute detail about her date.

Not his type of thing. He'd much rather discuss football, basketball, hunting season...Girl Scout cookies.

Anything but dud dates and pinching stilettos.

"See anything?" Taryn finally stopped her diatribe long enough to show some interest in the job.

"Nothing worth noting."

"I told you that there wouldn't be." Taryn opened the fridge and took out a can of diet soda. She'd changed into jeans and a T-shirt, braided her hair and scrubbed her face.

She still looked pretty, and nothing like what most people expected a security specialist to look like. But she was one of the best at the job, and he was glad to have her help.

"Hopefully, it will stay this quiet all night." Tessa needed a good night's sleep and a little peace. Maybe once she had that, she'd be more open to sharing her secrets.

And maybe flowers would bloom in the dead of winter.

He scowled, grabbed a soda from the fridge and

chugging half of it down with Advil. His shoulder was throbbing, but that was the least of his worries. He had to get the truth out of Tessa. It was the only way to help her.

Unfortunately, he wasn't sure she actually wanted to be helped.

"So," Taryn said, nudging him out of the way so she could grab a yogurt from the fridge. "Is she the new woman in your life?"

"Did I have an old one?" He diverted the question, because he wasn't sure how to answer. Tessa was part of his life. That was for sure. How much a part of it depended on her.

"Not that I know of. Which is why this situation is interesting."

"There's nothing interesting about it. She's my physical therapist. She ran into some trouble while I was at her office. I'm trying to help her out of it."

"Mmm-hmm." Taryn nodded, scooping up yogurt and watching him like he was the most interesting thing that had happened to her all day.

"What's that supposed to mean?"

"Nothing." She tossed the yogurt container and stuck the spoon in the dishwasher. "But, I'm thinking your evening has been a lot more interesting than mine, and I've got to admit, I'm a little jealous. So, what's the scoop on her troubles? An ex?"

"She's not saying much except that it's connected to her past." He explained briefly.

Taryn's eyes widened when he described the massacre. "Wow. That's a lot to go through. No wonder she's messed up."

"She's not messed up," he protested.

"Someone wants her dead. She probably knows who and why, but she's not saying. That's not messed up?"

"She has her reasons."

"And, *you've* got it bad." She smirked, but he didn't take the bait. Whatever he felt about Tessa was his business, and he wasn't going to discuss it with anyone. Especially not anyone as nosey as Taryn.

"How long do you plan to keep her here?" she finally asked.

"Good question. I'll have to discuss it with Tessa."

"There's no time like the present." Taryn sat at the kitchen table, tapping her fingers restlessly. "Besides, seeing as how I'm a woman, I speak with authority when I say that she probably isn't happy being in there alone. Not to mention the fact that she's probably starving. That's what happens to me when *I'm* bored." She grabbed a package of cookies from the cupboard and ate two.

"Are you trying to tell me you're bored?"

"I'm trying to give you some helpful relationship advice. Take it or leave it. It makes no difference to me."

"Relationship advice? Aren't you the woman who spent the evening with a dud?" He opened the fridge, grabbed everything he needed to make a couple sandwiches.

"Just because I date duds does not mean I don't know how a woman wants to be treated."

"You just don't know any men who know how to treat women that way?"

"Exactly." She laughed, just like he'd known she would.

He made a couple of sandwiches, dropped one onto a plate. "How's this?"

"A good start." She dismissed him with a wave of

her hand, turning her back to him and leaning over the computer monitor.

He didn't need an excuse to go talk to Tessa, but he took a sandwich to her room, anyway, knocking on the door and waiting impatiently for her to answer.

Someone rapped on the door, the hard knock making Tessa's heart jump. She hadn't been able to sleep. No matter how much she'd wanted to.

"Tess?" The doorknob rattled and Seth walked in. He had a plate in his hand and a smile on his face, and she couldn't remember the last time she'd been so happy to see someone.

"I brought you something to eat." He offered her the plate, and she took it, staring down at the sandwich, her heart beating double time.

It had been years since anyone had made her something to eat. So many years that she couldn't remember the last time it had happened.

"Thanks," she said, her eyes burning with what felt like tears. "But you really don't need to take care of me."

"Is that what giving someone a sandwich is?" He raised a brow, a hint of amusement in his eyes.

"Isn't it?"

"According to Taryn, the sandwich will help with boredom."

"You and Taryn were discussing me?"

"She's nosey," he said, settling into one of the chairs. "And she's helping us out, so I couldn't be too upset with her questions."

"I sound ungrateful, don't I?" She sat on the edge of the bed and set the plate on the bedside table. "I don't mean to. I really do appreciate what you're trying to do."

"You sound tired."

"I am, but I can't sleep."

"Maybe if you told me what's bothering you, it would help."

"The past." *And you,* she wanted to add, but didn't.

"I understand," he said quietly, and she thought that he did.

"You must miss your wife terribly."

"I do, but we were only meant to have the time we had. It took me a while to understand that. Once I did, her death was easier to accept."

"Accepting something doesn't make it easy," she said, forcing the words past the hard lump of grief in her throat.

"I didn't say it was easy. I said it was *easier,*" he corrected her, his eyes dark with emotion. "After Julia died, I had to make the choice to believe that the deepest darkness only exists to reveal the brightest light. Otherwise, I don't think I would have come home from Afghanistan."

"What kind of brightness did you find?" she asked, because she really wanted to know what had carried him through, brought him home, made him into the man he was.

"My family. They might drive me crazy, but they were there for me when I needed them. I stayed alive for them, and because I really believed God had a purpose for my life." He smiled, and Tessa's heart seemed to reach for his, the sensation so unexpected, so surprising, she stood and paced to the window.

Outside, fat flakes of snow fell against a background of steel-gray sky and deep-redbrick. She wanted to be outside, her face tilted to the cold night sky, white snow falling on her heated cheeks.

"There was something else, Tess," Seth said, moving up behind her, his hands settling on her shoulders, his breath ruffling her hair. "I knew that Julia wouldn't have wanted me to waste my life mourning her. She'd have wanted me to keep doing what we'd always planned."

"It's hard to do the things you planned with someone when they're gone."

"Not if what you planned was to have the best life you could, a life that honored God, that honored the people you love. It took me a couple of years, but I realized I could still do those things. Even without Julia in my life."

"You're a better person than I am, Seth. A stronger Christian."

"Obviously, you don't know me very well." He chuckled, the sound vibrating through her.

She turned to face him, found herself so close that she could feel his warmth, smell the crisp scent of soap and winter on his skin. "You're wrong. I do know you, and I know that you're a lot stronger than I could ever be."

"That's a copout, Tess. An excuse because you're afraid to try. Afraid God won't give you the things you want."

"I don't know what I want," she said, but she thought she might. She thought that everything she wanted might be standing right there in front of her.

Seth touched her cheek, his palm resting there, light as a summer breeze.

The air simmered with electricity, and Tessa's heart thundered in response. Breathless, she looked into his eyes and saw her own longing reflected in the depth of his gaze.

He stepped back, his jaw tight. "Eat your sandwich and try to sleep, Tessa. Tomorrow, we need to talk."

He walked into the hall, closing the door softly behind him. She heard the quiet click like thunder on a quiet morning.

Tomorrow, we need to talk.

About them?

About Tessa's past?

About the secrets she'd been keeping?

How much could she reveal without destroying everything the mission team had worked for?

How much did she want to reveal to Seth?

Everything, her heart whispered.

Nothing, her brain responded.

She grabbed the sandwich and ate it. She still felt empty. Hollow.

Alone.

She lay down, turning on her side to face the small nightstand that stood beside the bed. A thin Bible lay there, crowded between a lamp and the alarm clock. Black leather and well used, it reminded her of the one she'd inherited from her mother. A family Bible dating back nearly a hundred years, it had survived Tessa's parents' wild lives and had been handed to her the day she'd entered foster care. She'd left so many things behind over the years, but that Bible was one thing she always carried with her.

Sentimental value is what she'd told herself every time she'd packed it. There was more to it, though. The Bible represented what she'd wanted desperately to reclaim, the faith that should have carried her through the tough times but that seemed to constantly slip through her fingers.

She touched the Bible's black cover, wishing she were at home. She'd have dug out the family Bible, poured over words highlighted by generations of faith-filled people.

Her mother had fallen away from the foundation they'd laid for her. Tessa had done the same.

Could she find her way back?

Her soul yearned for that. She wanted to feel what she'd felt years ago—a sense of peace and love and belonging.

"Please, God, I just need to know You're there," she whispered.

She closed her eyes, hoping for some audible clue that she wasn't alone. She heard nothing, but she felt something stir to life deep in her soul, felt her heart acknowledge what she had denied for way too long.

God had never left her. He had always been as close as a whisper, as near as a prayer.

A phone rang, the soft sound drifting into the room.

One ring. Two. Seth's deep voice as he answered.

Seconds later, he knocked on the door.

"Tessa? Logan is on the phone. He has some information to share with you." He opened the door without waiting for a response, his expression grim.

"Bad news?" she asked as she took the phone.

"He wouldn't say."

She nodded, turning away before she could give in to the urge to throw herself into Seth's well-muscled arms. "Hello?"

"Tessa, it's Logan. I have some good news and some bad news." He paused, and she heard papers rustling. "The evidence team came up empty in your room."

"What's the good news?" she asked, wandering into the living room and settling onto the sofa, Seth following silently behind.

"We picked up three sets of fingerprints on the back door. We have matches for two of them—you and Seth. The third set, we've got no match for in the system. It wasn't there last time we dusted, though. Aside from you and Seth, has anyone been in the house with your permission?"

"No," she responded, her shoulders tense. A print with no match was about the same as nothing, but Logan seemed happy about it.

"Was your team fingerprinted when you went to Kenya?"

"I don't think so. Why?"

"Everything that's happening ties to that trip, Tessa. Something happened there. You're either aware of it—"

"I'm sorry, Logan, I've told you everything I can," she cut him off.

But, she hadn't told him everything she knew.

They both knew it.

"You can return home when you're ready," Logan said, obviously annoyed. "We'll keep a patrol car outside your house 24/7. Other than that, my hands are tied until we get a match on that print."

He disconnected, and Tessa handed Seth the phone, her cheeks blazing.

"He's…upset," she said lamely. She felt guilty, unhappy with her choice. Not sure how to change it. She'd been hiding things for so long, keeping quiet for so long. What she'd built with Daniel had seemed so much more important than the truth that she'd been hiding.

She wasn't sure he'd feel that way.

As a matter of fact, she was pretty sure that he wouldn't.

"Maybe Logan and I should start a club," Seth growled. "Men who aren't happy with you." He dropped the phone into his pocket and stalked into the kitchen, leaving her there, stewing in her own juices.

She wanted to follow him. Maybe apologize, but she

didn't know what to say. The weight of her secrets felt so much heavier than anything she could carry on her own.

She stayed where she was, her head pounding, her heart pounding with it. She felt sick and unhappy, and not sure what to do about it.

Seconds later, Seth returned, a glass of water in hand.

"Take this." He thrust it at her, and she grabbed it automatically.

"And these." He offered two pain relievers. "For your headache."

"I didn't say I had one," she pointed out, but she swallowed them down, anyway, because she *did* have a headache.

"You didn't have to. Just like you didn't have to say that you're hiding something for me to know that you are."

"Seth—"

"Someone is after you, Tessa. And I think you know who it is," he pronounced, a hard edge to his voice.

"I don't!" she protested, because that, at least, was the entire truth.

He studied her silently, his eyes cold. "Randal and I are working overtime to keep you safe while we try to figure out who's after you. You owe it to us to tell us what you know."

"If I knew who it was, I'd tell you." That was the truth, too.

"We're dealing with a guy who sneaks around to do his dirty work. Someone who wants the world to see him one way, but who isn't what he seems. A charlatan. Sound familiar?"

She almost said it didn't, because no one in her present life was like that.

But there *was* someone from her past.

An upright citizen on the surface but as evil as they came where it counted the most.

"What are you thinking?" Seth asked. He could tell Tessa was right on the edge of telling him something— something big.

"You just described my..."

"Your husband?" Seth couldn't imagine Tessa being in a relationship with someone who was pure on the surface and soul-deep dirty, but he'd known plenty of wonderful people who had made the mistake of believing the lies they were fed rather than the truth they experienced.

"No." She shook her head, her eyes flashing. "My brother-in-law. I thought Andrew was one of the kindest people I'd ever known. I found out after he died that everything he claimed to be was a lie."

"What happened?"

"I've already said too much." She started to move away but he grabbed her hand, holding her in place.

"You've barely said anything."

"I made a promise, Seth. I can't break it."

"To who?" he pressed. He had a feeling they were heading toward the truth she'd been hiding.

"I can't say." She pulled her hand from his. "I'm exhausted. I'm going to bed."

She ran down the hall and into her room, closing the door with enough force to shake a picture on the wall.

Taryn peeked out of the kitchen.

"Lover's quarrel?" she asked.

"Difference of opinion."

"Same thing, isn't it?"

"Tessa has information that could help us save her life. She doesn't want to reveal it."

"Why not?"

"She made a promise to someone."

"Promises become null and void when a life is on the line. Maybe you'd better tell her that."

She was right.

Seth knocked on Tessa's door and waited for her to open it.

ELEVEN

If there'd been a fire escape outside the window, Tessa would have been tempted to use it. After she'd told Seth about the promise she'd made, about the secret she was hiding, the last thing she wanted to do was open the door.

Seth knocked again.

"Ignoring me won't make me go away," he said.

Too bad, because she planned to ignore him awhile longer.

She should have kept her mouth shut about Andrew. Now she was going to have to do some damage control.

"Tessa?" He wiggled the doorknob.

She'd locked it.

For once, she was ahead of her problems.

But not that far ahead. Seth probably had a key. If not, she was sure he could find a way to unlock the door if he really wanted to.

She had a feeling he'd want to.

She glanced around the room, fighting the absurd urge to hide under the bed.

The doorknob wiggled again. "You better be decent, Tessa, because I'm coming in."

"Don't you dare—"

The door opened, and Seth stepped into the room.

"How did you do that!" she sputtered, her heart pounding double time.

"Easy." He glowered, his brows drawn together, his eyes flashing with irritation. "This is a safe house, Tessa. It's not safe if we can't get to our clients."

"I'm not your client."

"So you keep reminding me."

"It's true." She stood her ground, not backing up as Seth approached.

"Let me make this clear, okay? While you're here, you're going to be treated like a client. Clients do not lock themselves in rooms to avoid questions they don't want to answer. If they do, I open the door and keep right on asking."

"You can keep asking, but I can't answer your questions, so I guess we're at an impasse," she retorted, relieved that her voice didn't tremble, that she sounded as angry as he seemed to be.

"That's your choice, Tessa." He brushed hair from her neck, his fingers skimming over the fading bruises to make a point. "The problem is that you're in danger. Do you want to die with your secret? Or live without it? Because it seems to me, that's what all this is coming down to," he growled.

"I…"

"What?" He raked a hand through his hair. "Tell me, because I don't understand how anything can be as important as your life."

"There are plenty of things, plenty of *people* who are just as important."

"What people?"

"The mission spent two years planning and building a church and an orphanage in Kenya. From the day we met until the day he died, that was Daniel's life's goal. His parents were missionaries to Kenya when he was a kid, and he wanted to go back to serve the people there." She rubbed her arms, willing away the chill that settled deep in her bones every time she thought about Daniel and his dream.

"And?" Seth pulled the comforter from the end of the bed and wrapped it around her shoulders, the gesture so sweet that her heart skipped a beat.

"I don't want anything to happen to what he and the rest of the mission team built."

"Here's the thing, Tessa." He leaned down so they were eye to eye, their foreheads nearly touching, his hands on her shoulders. "I don't want anything to happen to *you*."

"Seth, please, just let it go," she whispered, her throat so tight she could barely get the words out.

"If I do, you could end up dead, and I could end up blaming myself. I'm not willing to go through that again."

He cared, and cared deeply.

She could see it in his eyes, hear it in the gentleness of his voice

She cared, too. More than she should. She was almost willing to sacrifice everything for a chance to have what she saw in Seth's eyes.

She looked away, her heart hammering in her chest, her eyes burning with tears, because she knew what Daniel would have done. He would have given up the dream for the sake of the truth. He would have trusted God to build what needed to be built. With or without his help.

"Jack Dempsey asked me not to say anything. He knows what happened in Kenya," she said, hot tears spilling down her cheeks. In all the years that she'd held the truth close, she'd never considered doing anything but what Jack had asked of her. Now, she thought that maybe she should have been considering a lot of other things.

She wiped at the tears, surprised by them. Uncomfortable, because Seth was seeing them.

"Who is he?" Seth asked.

He didn't touch her, and she was glad, because if he had, the tears might have turn to sobs, and then she might not have been able to speak at all. "The head of the mission board that sent our team to Kenya."

"Why did he ask you to keep quiet?"

"He was afraid that bad press would stop the donations that started pouring in after the massacre. If that happened, thousands of lives would have been affected."

"What kind of bad press?"

"He thought that someone on the mission team was responsible for the massacre. That his actions had angered the insurgents and caused them to attack us."

"Your brother-in-law?"

"Yes."

She walked to the window, staring out at the snow. She wanted to feel good about what she'd done, wanted to feel as if Daniel would approve.

She just felt hollow and old.

"I have to call Logan and give him the information. You know that, right?" Seth said quietly.

"Yes." Her voice broke, and she blinked away more tears.

"It's going to be okay, Tessa."

"You can't know that."

"Sure I can." He tugged her into his arms, pressed her head to his chest. "If God is in it, it can't *not* be."

"What if He's *not* in it? What if I've just made a huge mistake?"

"You haven't." The words rumbled beneath Tessa's ear, Seth's heart beating steadily. He was so different from Daniel. Solid and muscular where Daniel had been narrow and lean; calm and steady where Daniel had been hyper and driven.

She had a feeling that Seth would love his wife above everything except for God. She had a feeling that when he made a commitment to someone, it would never be overshadowed by his commitment to something else.

She clutched Seth's shirt, hating that she was comparing Daniel to him. Hating it even more that Daniel was coming up short.

She forced herself to step away, afraid that if she didn't, she really would start sobbing. "I'm really tired, Seth. Can we talk more about this in the morning?"

"Sure." He touched her cheek, looking deep into her eyes.

She didn't know what he was searching for, or if he found it. She just knew that she could have stood there with him forever, could have waited a lifetime to find out what he was going to say.

Finally, he turned away without a word, left the room and closed the door.

She turned off the light and crawled into bed fully clothed, the comforter still around her shoulders, tears streaming down her cheeks again. She hadn't cried in years. Now, she couldn't seem to stop.

She closed her eyes, listening to the storm outside the window, wishing the sounds would drown out her memories and her fear.

She'd told Seth things that she'd never told anyone

else. She couldn't take that back, couldn't steal back the words and hide them away again.

She wasn't sure she'd have wanted to, even if she could.

Go. Don't look back.

Those were the last words Daniel had spoken to her. She'd never forgotten them. They'd followed her for five years, and she thought they'd probably follow her for the rest of her life.

She'd always believed that he'd been telling her to leave the village, urging her to go in case the insurgents returned.

But he hadn't seemed frantic. Even near death, he'd been at peace, concerned for her rather than for himself.

Maybe he'd known how difficult it would be for her to move on. Maybe he'd realized how much she'd struggle. Maybe he'd wanted his final words to be ones that would send her into the future without regrets.

If that were the case, she'd really messed things up. Instead of heading into the future, she'd clung to the past, keeping a secret that had tied her to all the things that she most needed to let go of.

A soft sobbed escaped, and she pressed her face to the pillow, muffling the sound until she finally fell asleep.

TWELVE

The sun rose sharp and bright outside the apartment building, its golden glow gleaming on the dark hardwood floor and drilling into Seth's eyes.

He wasn't happy about it. It had been a long night, and after four hours of sleep, he wasn't quite ready to be awake.

He grabbed a mug from the cupboard and poured coffee into it, gulping down a mouthful that scalded the back of his throat.

"You should have waited for it to cool," Taryn said dryly, her fingers tapping restlessly on the kitchen countertop.

"I need my brain cells functioning. Caffeine is the quickest way to make that happen."

"You could have had the green-tea smoothie I offered you. Are you sure you don't want me to make you one?" She took a sip of hers, shuddering slightly.

"Seeing as how you're nearly gagging that down, I think I'll pass."

"It's not that bad." She took another sip, set the glass down. "Then again, maybe coffee wouldn't be so bad."

"Told you." He laughed, glancing at the stove clock, then down the hall to Tessa's closed door. They had a lot to discuss—even more than he'd imagined when he'd left her room last night. "Think she plans on getting up anytime soon?"

Taryn shrugged, her braided hair bouncing. "Why don't you go knock on the door and ask?"

"I don't want to wake her."

"Sure you do," she said with a smirk.

She was right. He did. He just wasn't sure he *should*.

He scowled into his coffee cup, his shoulder aching dully. Payback for the lift down the stairs that he'd given Tessa.

"So, does she usually sleep until—" Taryn glanced at the clock "—nine?"

"I don't know."

"So go find out. Knock on the door. Ask if she's awake. You know, do normal, everyday things that normal people do, because I have a hair appointment at ten, and I'm not planning to miss it."

"You can go."

"You two need to be out before I leave. That's the rule."

"Sometimes rules are meant to be broken," he griped.

"Obviously, you woke up on the wrong side of the bed." Taryn took another sip of her smoothie and frowned at the glass. "Tastes like grass."

"I'm sure it does."

"As soon you leave, I can dump it out and get some OJ."

"Why wait?"

"Because I don't want a witness to my crime. Go!" She shooed him out of the kitchen, and he went, because it was past time to knock on Tessa's door. Make sure she was okay. Tell her what he'd learned from Logan.

He rapped on her door, shifting his weight impatiently.

"Hold on!" Tessa called, her voice muffled and faint.

An image flashed through his head—Tessa, pink-cheeked from sleep, her eyes hazy with dreams.

The door opened and she appeared, eyes red-rimmed, damp hair pulled back, skin pale. The scent of flowers and berries drifted around her, the aroma as compelling as sunlight on a winter morning. He wanted to touch her silky cheek, feel the warmth of her skin beneath his hand.

Take her in his arms again, hold her like he had last night. Having her in his arms had felt like coming home—comfortable and comforting with just an edge of something fantastic and new. He wouldn't have minded experiencing that again, and it took everything he had not to reach for her.

Tessa felt electricity in the air and instinctively took a step back, her cheeks flushed.

"Sorry for the wait. I thought a shower would wash some of the fog from my brain," she explained even though he hadn't asked. She felt nervous, edgy, anxious. She wanted to say that lack of sleep had caused it, but she knew better.

Seth was the reason.

His eyes. His voice. *Him.*

"Did it?" he asked, his voice husky.

"No. I think I need a few more hours of sleep for that. Or a cup of coffee." Tessa sidled past, careful not to brush against him.

She'd learned a hard lesson from Andrew about people not being what they said they were, and trust didn't come easily for her. But even after a long night of trying to convince herself that Seth wasn't what he seemed, she still wanted to trust him.

She *did* trust him.

Because nothing could change the facts. Everything he'd done, everything he'd said, had been a reflection of his heart.

And his heart was pretty amazing.

She caught a whiff of coffee and aftershave as they walked down the hall, and it reminded her of long lazy mornings and conversations across the breakfast table. A million butterflies took flight in her stomach, and she had to force herself not to turn and reach for him.

She hurried the rest of the way into the kitchen, stopping a few feet away from Taryn.

"What's the rush?" Taryn looked up from the computer screen and frowned.

"I need coffee." And distance from Seth. A continent's worth of distance might be appropriate. She opened a cupboard, searching for a coffee cup, her hands shaking for reasons she didn't want to name.

"In here." Seth reached above her and handed her a white mug, their fingers brushing.

"Thanks," she said, pouring coffee, searching the refrigerator for cream, doing everything she could think of to put off meeting Seth's eyes.

She'd been in his arms, her head pressed to his chest, his heart beating beneath her ear. And, she wouldn't have minded being there again.

And again and again.

That scared her. A lot.

"This place has been dead quiet all night," Taryn said, cutting through the tension. "I don't know about the two of you, but I'm about ready to get out of here."

"I feel the same. It'll be good to get home," Tessa responded as she halfheartedly stirred her coffee.

"I'm not sure home is the best place for you," Seth said.

"I can't think of any place that would be better. Besides, Bentley is coming home from the vet today. He's a good deterrent." She looked up from her coffee, steeling herself as she met Seth's eyes. They were dark blue and rimmed with shadows, his face scruffy with a five-o'clock shadow. "Did you call Logan last night?"

"I did." He refilled his coffee, took a sip and didn't say another word.

"And?" she prodded.

"We can discuss it now—" he glanced at Taryn "—or, we can discuss it on the way to the vet. It's up to you."

He was worried about sharing private information in front of Taryn.

Of course he was.

His heart, again. And she just couldn't seem to resist it.

Or him.

"We can discuss it on the way to the vet," she replied, dropping her gaze and making a production out of looking at her watch. "I was supposed to be at Amy's early, but I guess I've missed the boat on that."

"If you're ready, we can go now." Seth placed his mug in the sink.

"I'm ready." She took a last long sip of coffee and did the same, her arm brushing against his.

He stilled, his gaze dropping to her lips. The kitchen fading away. Everything faded away but Seth.

Heat shot up her cheeks, her heart thrumming crazily.

She had to get Seth out of her life.

Or throw herself into his arms.

One or the other, and she wasn't sure which she wanted more.

"Can you two stop staring into each other's eyes and get this show on the road?" Taryn said dryly. "If

I don't get my hair straightened today, it's going to be like sheep's wool by tomorrow."

Her voice was the splash of ice water Tessa needed to tear her gaze away from Seth's.

"I'll get my bag," she muttered and ran into the bedroom to grab it. The sooner they left, the sooner she could hear what Logan had said about Jack.

It had been years since Tessa had had any contact with the mission board director. She'd always assumed that he'd kept track of her, though. To be honest, she'd always thought that he was the person behind the roses.

A reminder of the secret they'd shared.

She pressed her lips together and kept silent as Seth and Taryn escorted her to the truck. The storm had broken hours ago, but the air was bitter and cold, the bright sun adding little warmth.

Tessa shivered as Seth helped her into the truck.

He pulled off his coat, tucking it around her.

"Now you're going to be cold," she chided.

"I'll live." He shut her in, rounded the truck and spoke quietly to Taryn for a minute before he slid into the driver's seat. "All right. We're set. Let's go pick up your mutt. Which direction are we heading?"

"West on I-90, and Bentley is not a mutt."

"Then what is he?"

"A cherished member of the family."

"I hope that your cherished family member can fit in the backseat, because I don't think there's going to be room for him up here."

"He'll fit."

"Without chewing the leather?"

"He doesn't chew anything but dog food," she responded. But she wasn't concerned with how well Bentley would fit in the truck. She was worried about what

Logan had said about Jack. "You said that you spoke to Logan?" she prodded.

"I called him last night. He called me back this morning. They tracked down Jack Dempsey." He glanced her way, his eyes dark with something she wasn't sure she wanted to know about.

"Where is he?"

"Dead."

She flinched at his words, pulling his coat tighter around her shoulders, wrapping herself in his warmth and scent. "When did he die?"

"Last year. He was shot during what police believed was a botched robbery attempt at his home in Houston."

"They *believed* it was a botched robbery attempt?"

"There's some new evidence, and they may reopen the case."

"What kind of evidence?"

"Jack was murdered on the fourth anniversary of the massacre."

She went cold at his words, her heart skipping a beat. "Are you sure?"

"I'm afraid so. I'm sorry, Tess."

"Me, too," she said.

Seth touched her hand, his finger brushing across her knuckles so lightly she should have barely felt the contact. Instead, it warmed her like liquid fire, made her want to lay her head on his shoulder, close her eyes, let him take care of everything.

Such a silly thought.

"Tessa, tell me what happened with your brother-in-law," he said quietly.

She didn't want to talk about Andrew, hated to even think about what he'd done, but what choice did he have?

Jack was dead. There was no way that his death—on

the anniversary of the massacre—was a coincidence. Had he been killed because of what he knew? Was it possible that someone had survived the massacre and come to the States seeking revenge? A villager? A teenager who was now an adult? Someone who blamed the mission group for the tragedy that Andrew had brought down on the village?

"Logan and I agreed that anything you tell us will be kept in confidence." Seth broke into her thoughts. "He'll keep the investigation as quiet as he can, but it's time, Tessa. We have to know what your brother-in-law did."

She took a deep breath, trying to calm her racing heart. "After the massacre, I found out that he'd embezzled funds from the mission and hired children from a school we were running to mine diamonds. He paid their families to keep quiet. When he died, he had a million dollars in a Kenyan bank."

"That's a terrible crime, Tessa, but it isn't something that the mission board would be held responsible for."

"There's more. The insurgents who attacked the village were retaliating. Andrew's crew was working in diamond mines that belonged to them. Because of his greed, twenty innocent people were killed or wounded."

Seth whistled softly.

"Exactly," she murmured, staring out the side window, her eyes hot and dry. Seth took her hand, twining his fingers through hers. "It's not your fault."

"Then why does it feel like it is?"

"Because you think there must have been some sign you missed, some way for you to know who Andrew really was. You think that if you'd seen it, you could have prevented everything that happened."

He was right. She'd spent five years thinking she could have prevented the massacre. Five years believing that if she'd just been smart enough, no one would have died. Not even Daniel.

"Maybe I could have," she whispered, and Seth squeezed her hand, his thumb running across her wrist.

"Nothing you could have done would have changed anything, Tess. It's time to believe that and move on."

He was right about that, too, but she couldn't speak past the lump in her throat, couldn't tell him how much lighter she felt.

Sharing the burden she'd carried had freed something inside her, loosened the chains that had held her to the past, given her a chance to have what she'd wanted all along—a fresh start, a new beginning.

A life lived out from under the long shadow of Andrew's crime.

She wanted it so badly that her heart raced with the thought, her muscles tense and stiff with it.

"You okay?" Seth asked, and she nodded, because her throat was still too tight to speak, and because nothing she could say would compare to what she felt. Hope. Faith. Trust. All of it rolled into a ball of longing that lodged in her throat and stayed there as they made their way toward Amy's veterinary clinic.

THIRTEEN

Seth let Tessa have her silence.

He understood her regrets and her guilt.

He also understood how useless both were. Carrying them around couldn't change what had happened. It could only keep her from moving forward. He'd told her that. What she did with it was up to her.

"Turn here," Tessa said, her voice thick and hot. She wasn't crying, but he wouldn't be surprised if she did. She'd been through a lot, and it wasn't over yet. It wouldn't be over until they found the person responsible for her troubles.

He took the turn she'd indicated, the road narrowing, deep forest pressing in on either side. Bits of snow and ice still clung to towering pine trees but the storm had cleared, watery sunlight dappling the dark pavement. A beautiful fall morning, but danger could be hiding around the bend. He had to keep that in mind, and stay focused on keeping Tessa safe.

"I need to call Logan and give him the information you've provided," he said, reluctantly releasing Tessa's hand.

"I know."

"He's a good guy, Tessa. He'll do everything he can

to keep the information from becoming the news story of the week."

"I hope it's enough. There are plenty of people who would love to make Andrew a poster child for why Christian organizations can't be trusted. If one national news syndicate gets wind of it…"

"Don't borrow trouble. It'll only make you miserable."

"I've had nothing *but* trouble since I went to Kenya, so, trust me, I'm not even tempted to borrow it." She sighed. "Amy's clinic is the next right."

He made the turn, following a narrow driveway out of the pine forest and into open farmland. Several horses munched hay in one field, a few lamas interspersed among them. Another field held several alpaca and a donkey that brayed loudly as Seth drove by. As far as the eye could see, animals dotted the landscape. Tessa's friend Amy seemed to be doing well for herself as a veterinarian.

The driveway emptied out into a large parking lot. Beyond it, a one-story brick building stretched across a wide yard. Seth pulled up close to the building and parked the car.

Tessa reached for the door handle, but he grabbed her hand. "I want to call Logan first. The sooner he starts looking into your brother-in-law's life and death, the better."

She settled back into her seat, her face pale, her eyes red-rimmed with fatigue. "I don't know what good it will do to investigate Andrew. He's been dead for five years."

"He was killed during the massacre, right?" He dialed Logan's number as he spoke, scanning the quiet parking lot while he waited.

"Kidnapped. He was killed a few days later."

"He was—"

Logan picked up, cutting off the rest of Seth's question.

"Deputy Sheriff Randal," he said, his voice curt and rushed.

"It's Seth. I have some more information for you." He stared into Tessa's eyes as he spoke. She didn't flinch, didn't blink, didn't give away her feelings, but he could feel her regret and anxiety.

"Go ahead."

Seth explained briefly, sure that somehow Andrew Camry was the key to everything that was happening. Someone had known about his crimes and had wanted revenge enough to travel halfway around the world to get it.

"Is Tessa there?" Logan asked.

"Yes."

"Let me speak to her." It was an order more than a request, but Seth handed her the phone, anyway. He and Logan had been working well together, and he didn't want to change the dynamics by irritating the guy.

"Hello?" Tessa said reluctantly. She didn't really want to speak with Logan, but she knew there was no way to avoid it. Pandora's box had been opened, and all kinds of horrible things were flying out of it.

"How are you doing this morning?" Logan asked.

"I'm still alive," she said.

Logan didn't laugh.

"Good. That's what we want. That's our goal and our focus. You understand that, right, Tessa?"

"I'm not a child, Logan. You don't have to pat me on the head and tell me what a good job I've done in order to keep me cooperating."

"That wasn't my intention," he said, then sighed. "Okay, maybe it was, but you gave Seth some good information. I need more."

"What do you want to know?"

"Andrew was kidnapped during the massacre?"

"Yes."

"His body was found a few days later?"

"No. His body was found two years later." She'd been in the States by then, already aware of what he'd done. She hadn't mourned him. "Based on the condition of his remains, the police theorized that he'd been killed within days of the massacre."

"The medical examiner positively identified the remains?" Logan pressed.

"No. It wasn't possible. His body had been buried in a shallow grave and dug up by animals. There were only a few bones remaining, but his wallet was there and the shirt he'd been wearing." Bile filled her throat at the words, and she swallowed it down. She hadn't mourned Andrew, but she wouldn't have wished his fate on her worst enemy.

"Convenient," Seth muttered.

"So," Logan said, oblivious to the comment, "it's possible your brother-in-law is alive."

Her heart jumped at his words, her stomach churning. No way could Andrew be alive.

"Tess?" Logan pressed. "Is it possible?"

"No.

"There is no hard evidence that he's dead, though, right?

"His wallet—"

"Anyone could have put that with the remains. Even him."

Could Andrew have survived?

She didn't want to think so. Didn't want to even consider it, but she couldn't stop wondering, imagining, thinking about what it would be like if he *had* survived.

"Tessa?" Seth touched her hand. "You okay?"

She wasn't, but she nodded.

"If Andrew survived, he's the only one who knows it," she finally managed to say.

"How many other people survived?" Logan asked.

"Ninety villagers. One missionary."

"Do you know the name?"

"Anna Goodwin. She'd only been there for a couple weeks before the massacre." The night of the murders, Tessa had found Anna stumbling from her hut and had nearly carried her from the village, darkness pressing around them.

If she let herself, she could still hear Anna's screams. Hear the sobs of the mothers and fathers and children they passed by. Still smell the coppery scent of blood that had seeped into packed earth and stained the ground.

She gagged, handing the phone to Seth. "I need some air."

She yanked the truck door open and tumbled out into the cold, her brow beaded with sweat, her face hot.

She heard Seth's door open and close, knew he was following as she made her way to the clinic.

He snagged the back of her coat before she reached it, tugging her around and into his arms.

He felt warm and strong and so much more familiar than she wanted him to be.

"It's okay," he murmured against her hair.

She stood there for a moment, inhaling his scent, absorbing his warmth. It felt good.

Too good.

She stepped away, smoothing her hair, hoping Seth didn't notice the way her hands trembled. "I need to get Bentley."

Seth tucked a strand of hair behind her ear, his fingers calloused and rough but his touch as warm and light as a summer breeze. "Logan is going to meet us at your place. He needs more information. The best thing you can do is give it to him."

"I will."

"Good." He smiled gently and wrapped his arm around her waist. "Now, let's go get that giant mutt of yours."

"He is not a mutt," she protested, and he chuckled, the sound chasing away some of the horror and sadness that thinking about Kenya always brought.

The clinic door opened, and Amy stepped outside. "Are you two planning to stay out here all day, or are you coming in to get Bentley? Because I'm pretty sure he knows you're here. He's been whining and scratching at the kennel door for five minutes."

"We're coming," Tessa replied quickly, breaking away from Seth and going to the door. Bentley she could deal with. Seth she wasn't so sure about. If she stayed in his arms too long, if she thought too much about how it felt to be there, she might never want to leave.

"I was expecting you earlier," Amy said in her normal blunt fashion. She'd pulled her dark hair into a bun at the back of her head, and her glasses were perched on the end of her nose. She looked more like a schoolmarm than a veterinarian. "It's a busy day, so we'll have to hurry up."

"I'm sorry about the delay. I've been dealing with… trouble."

Amy glanced at Seth and scowled. "I can see that."

"Not him!"

"Sure. When there is a man involved it's always trouble. I learned that the hard way. Come on." She led them past a receptionist's desk and into the kennel. "Bentley is doing well. His hip is healing nicely. No running for the next few weeks, and I'll want to see him the day after tomorrow."

"That's fine," Tessa replied, and a dog howled frantically in reply.

"I think that might be your cherished family member," Seth offered as they rounded a corner and walked through an aisle lined with kennels.

"He can't help it that he's loud. He has a big voice to go with his big body."

Seth laughed, the sound shivering along her spine and lodging deep in her heart. It filled an empty spot that she hadn't realized was there, offered more than she'd been looking for. More than she'd thought she would ever have again.

"All right, you beast. You're free," Amy said affectionately as she opened Bentley's kennel.

The dog lunged toward Tessa as if his life depended on getting to her, his tongue lolling out of his mouth, his one good ear perked up with excitement.

Tessa crouched to greet him, rubbing his knobby head, and accepted his slobbery kisses.

"All right. Enough." She nudged him back and hooked him to the leash that Amy offered. "Thanks for taking care of him, Amy."

"It's my job. Besides, I like the big lug. You've already paid in full, so I'll let you three show yourselves out. I have patients waiting." Amy hurried away, and Seth took Bentley's leash.

"Let's get out of here. Logan is probably already

waiting at your place." He pressed his hand to her lower back, and Tessa could feel his palm through her coat and shirt.

They walked out of the clinic that way, and if Tessa hadn't known better, if she'd been standing on the outside looking in, she'd have thought they were a couple. Two people picking up their beloved family pet together.

She wasn't sure how she felt about that, but she couldn't deny how wonderful it was to have someone to lean on. Someone beside her. After so many years of facing her fears and troubles alone, she had someone who wanted to face them with her.

It was a heady feeling. One she could give into completely if she let herself. But she didn't want to let herself. She didn't want to be heartbroken again, forced to create something out of the ashes of her dreams again.

"Don't look so scared, Tessa," Seth said as he opened the truck door. "I'm not going to let anything happen to you."

"I'm not worried about something happening to me," she responded, her voice huskier than it should have been.

"You should be," he responded as he slid his arms under Bentley's stomach.

"Don't! You're going to wreck your shoulder. Let me get him." She put a hand on his arm, his biceps bulging beneath her fingers as he did exactly what she'd told him not to. "I told you—"

"It's already done. So how about you climb in and we get moving?" he grumbled, his eyes flashing with irritation, pain or, more likely, both.

"Fine, but as your physical therapist—"

"In case I haven't made it clear," he cut in, "I'm not all that interested in having you as a physical therapist."

"You need rehab," she protested as she climbed into the truck.

"There are other things I need, too," he said.

She didn't plan to ask him what those things were.

She thought she probably already knew.

She grabbed the door handle, planning to pull it shut.

Seth held it open. "Aren't you going to ask what they are?"

"No."

"Chicken."

"I think we've already established that."

"Then, maybe it's time we establish *this*." He leaned down, his lips brushing hers so gently, she barely felt them, and yet they were all she *could* feel, all she knew. Just that moment, that brief touch. It made her want to move closer, it made her want more than she should.

Need more than she thought she could ever have.

It was the path to destruction, but she couldn't seem to pull away. Not when his hands slid down her arms. Not when they were palm to palm, fingers entwined. Not when Seth tugged her closer, made her forget every reason why she shouldn't be in his arms.

A car pulled into the parking lot, the roar of the engine cutting through the moment.

Seth broke away, his breathing uneven, his eyes blazing.

"I'm not going to apologize," he said gruffly, closing the door and rounding the car.

He met her eyes as he slid behind the wheel.

"I won't the next time, either," he said.

Next time?

Did he really think there'd be one?

Did she?

Did she want a next time?

Bentley whined, his dark head resting on the back-seat.

She turned, murmuring to the dog and hoping that Seth would start the engine, take off and not say another word about the kiss, or his feelings on the subject.

She had enough to deal with.

She didn't need to throw a relationship on top of it.

Her life had been routine and mundane, exactly the way she liked it. Now, it seemed to be chaos. And right in the middle of it all was Seth. The calm in the midst of the storm. Even with his sweet kisses and his gruff commands.

She clenched her fists, absolutely refusing to meet his eyes.

"Logan is waiting. Shouldn't we go?" she prodded, but Seth didn't start the engine.

"You can't avoid looking at me forever," he chided.

"I can try," she muttered, but she met his eyes, her breath catching. "We do have to go."

"I want to make sure that you know this isn't over."

"This?"

"Us. Whatever we have, it's something I'm not planning to run from."

"I…"

"No need to comment, Tessa." He backed out of the parking spot and pulled onto the road, a look of determination on his face.

She should have told him that they didn't have anything. That they would never have anything.

But she didn't believe it herself, and she wouldn't lie. Not to him, and not to herself.

There was something between them, and it seemed to

grow every time they looked into each other's eyes. She couldn't deny it, but she couldn't put a name to it, either.

Not now.

Maybe not ever.

But that didn't mean she couldn't enjoy the moment and allow herself to imagine—just for a while—that things could work out with Seth Sinclair.

FOURTEEN

Logan was leaning against the porch railing when they arrived at the house. Hat in hand and scowl on his face, he looked about as happy to be kept waiting as Seth was to be bringing Tessa back to her place.

He wanted her in the safe house under lock and key.

Based on her silence during the ride, he'd say she wasn't all that interested in what he wanted. The kiss had changed things between them—there was no doubt about that. He didn't regret it, but he wasn't going to let it get in the way of keeping her safe, either.

He pulled into Tessa's driveway and parked behind her Mustang. "I'll come around—"

She didn't give him a chance to finish.

She was out of the truck, cajoling Bentley to try to get him to get out before Seth even opened his door.

He jogged to her side of the vehicle and nudged her out of the way. "I'll get him. You go inside."

"I can—"

"Tessa, you're out in the open. You may as well just pin a target to your shirt," he cut in.

"He's right," Logan agreed, taking Tessa's arm and hurrying to the house. "Until we figure out what's going on, we can't be too careful."

They disappeared inside the house, and Seth turned his attention to Bentley. The mutt licked his hand, but didn't budge.

"Come on, dog. You're home. Let's go." He reached into the backseat, his shoulder straining as he maneuvered the dog out the door and set him on the ground.

Bentley's tail swished, but he didn't seem eager to move.

"Let's go." Seth gave the leash a light tug, and Bentley lumbered toward the house, his nose raised as he sniffed the air. They were a yard from the porch step when he stopped in his tracks and growled deep in his throat. Hackles raised, he lunged toward the back of the house.

Seth let him have the lead, running through the backyard and up the hill that led into the woods.

Someone shouted behind him. Logan maybe, but he didn't want to take the time to answer. If the perp was up on the hill again, he planned to find him.

"Seth! Hold up!" Logan called.

This time there was no ignoring him.

"Move faster!" Seth barked, following Bentley onto a path that led through the thick pine forest. A half a mile in and Bentley didn't slow, his one good ear standing straight up as he pursued the trail.

Logan raced up behind them, his heavy breathing joining Seth's in breaking the stillness of the forest. "What's going on?"

"Bentley went crazy when he got out of the truck. He scented someone. I think it's our guy."

"Or it could have been a deer, a cat, a kid."

"No way. He's out here. I can feel it." The energy was there, the feeling that somewhere just out of sight, someone was watching. He'd felt it hundreds of times in Afghanistan, and he couldn't ignore it.

They ran another mile, cresting the rise of the hill and following it down to the river. Bentley slowed, sniffing at the underbrush, the tension easing from his body. Finally, he sat on his haunches, shook his head and looked as if he planned to stay there awhile.

"Looks like he lost the trail," Logan said as he scanned the area. "I'm going to look around. There are a couple of dirt roads that bisect these woods. It's possible he drove in and walked the rest of the way."

"Sounds good. I'll head south."

Logan frowned. "I don't think so, Sinclair. You're not a police officer, and that could get us both into a lot of trouble. I'm calling in a couple of deputies to help. You should go back to the house and keep an eye on Tessa until I get back."

It wasn't Seth's first choice but the thought of Tessa alone at the house, made him nod. "I'll head back. Keep me posted. Come on, Bentley. Let's go home."

The big dog lumbered to his feet, limping slightly as they walked back the way they'd come. Tessa wouldn't be happy that Seth had let the dog run pell-mell up the hill.

Seth wouldn't be happy if something had happened to Tessa while he was out on the trail.

He frowned, anxiety crawling along his spine.

What better way to get to someone than to distract the people protecting her? It was security 101. Never leave your client unprotected.

He had.

Logan had.

For all either of them knew, the perp had circled around and headed back to the house.

The thought left him cold, and he tightened his grip on Bentley's leash, breaking into a sprint as they barreled down the hill toward Tessa's house.

Tessa spread several blankets on the floor in front of the fireplace, tossed an oversize pillow down with them and stood back to survey the bed she was making for Bentley.

He'd love it, but she wanted to keep adding blankets and pillows. Not because Bentley needed them, but because she needed to keep busy. Seth and Logan had run off twenty minutes ago, and she hadn't heard a word from either of them since. Plus, they had her dog. If she hadn't been so afraid, she'd have gone looking for them, and when she'd found them, she would have let them have it for allowing Bentley to run after he'd just had surgery.

She *was* afraid, though.

Terrified.

The old house groaned as she walked into the kitchen and filled the teakettle. She'd heard the same creaking sigh hundreds of times before and thought nothing about it. Now, it sounded sinister. Like footsteps in the attic. Stealthy movement at the top of the stairs. Her heart raced at the thought, her stomach sick with terror.

Someone rapped on the back door, and Tessa jumped, whirling toward the mudroom as if someone were about to crash through the outside door and race into the house.

Another sharp knock split the eerie silence.

She grabbed a steak knife and crept into the room. There were no windows in the door, and she couldn't see who was standing on the other side of it.

Whoever it was could have a gun, a knife, a—

"Tessa? Open up. It's Seth."

Weak with relief, she fumbled with the lock, yanked the door open and nearly threw herself into his arms. She might have if Bentley hadn't nosed his way in between them.

"Thank goodness you're okay! I've been worried sick," she cried.

"Yeah? So have I." He nudged Bentley out of the way and walked into the mudroom, shaking his head as he caught sight of the steak knife.

"Would you really have been able to use it?" he asked, taking it from her hand and heading into the kitchen to set it on the counter.

"I hope so," she replied, following him.

The next thing she knew, she was in his arms, her face buried in his coat, her hands clutching his sides. She wasn't even sure how she'd gotten there, but he smelled like pine needles and crisp fall air, and he felt like home.

Her throat tightened at the thought, her eyes filling with tears. Such a silly thing to cry about.

She stepped back, cleared her throat and looked into his face. Not average at all. Exceptional—everything about him.

And she wasn't sure what to do with that, or how to react to it.

For now, she wouldn't react at all. She'd deal with the issue at hand. Seth and Logan running off into the woods and leaving her wondering what had happened and if they were okay.

"What happened?" she asked. "Logan said that Bentley took off."

"He must have caught someone's scent. We followed the trail for a couple of miles and finally lost it near the river." He raked his hand through his hair, his frustration obvious. "I thought the guy might have circled back around and come here."

"He didn't, and I'm fine." But she wanted the nightmare to end, wanted to stop feeling stalked and watched and afraid.

"But what if you weren't?" Seth took her hand, pressed a kiss to her knuckles. "I can't let anything happen to you, Tessa. I think you should stay at the safe house until this is over. "

"What if it never is? I can't stay there forever."

"You can't run forever, either," he responded quietly.

Bentley woofed and nosed his empty bowls.

A good distraction, and Tessa latched onto it, hurrying to fill his food and water bowls. Anything to avoid continuing the conversation.

Seth leaned against the kitchen counter, his coat open, his faded jeans clinging to muscular thighs. He looked tired, his eyes deeply shadowed. He'd thrown himself into protecting her. She couldn't ignore that any more than she could ignore him.

She sighed, shoving loose strands of hair behind her ears. "I'm not planning on running," she finally said, because staying really was her only option. Going into hiding, changing her name, none of those things would solve her problems. And she *needed* to solve them if she was ever going to move on with her life.

It was time to do that.

Past time.

The doorbell rang, pealing through the house and breaking into the conversation.

"That's probably Logan. Stay here. Just in case it's not." Seth walked out of the room.

She poured hot water over a tea bag and started the

coffeepot, the sound of voices carrying into the room. Logan's voice. Seth's. They'd both have dozens of questions for her to answer.

For once, she didn't mind. She'd already shared her darkest secrets. There was nothing more to hide.

Footsteps sounded on the hardwood floor, and the men walked into the room. Her heart jumped as she met Seth's eyes.

"Are you making coffee?" Logan queried. "Because I could sure use a cup."

"It will be ready in a minute." She took two mugs from the cupboard, her cheeks heating as Seth slipped them from her hands.

"You're flushed," he said. "Everything okay?"

"I was just wondering if Logan found anything out in the woods," she responded, retreating to the table and waiting while the men got their coffee.

"Nothing." Logan settled in the chair to her left. "But there's an old service road near where Bentley lost the trail. I left an officer there searching for evidence."

"I hope he finds something." Tess touched Bentley's head, the silky warmth of his fur comforting.

"Me, too," Logan replied. "For right now, though, I'd like to ask you a few more questions."

"That's fine," she responded. She wanted to cooperate. She needed to give Logan everything he asked for, but she still felt nervous, the idea of discussing Kenya and Andrew's betrayal as uncomfortable as ever.

Seth touched her hand, offered an easy smile, and all the nerves seemed to slip away.

"Thanks," Logan said, taking a sip of coffee. "I know we're all tired, so I'll try to make it quick. You mentioned Anna Goodwin when we spoke earlier."

"Yes."

"I ran a search on her name and was able to trace her to a small town a hundred miles north of Houston. She moved there after she recovered from the injuries she sustained during the massacre."

"Her parents told me that when I tried to get in touch with her after we returned home. They said she didn't want anything to do with anyone from Kenya."

Logan nodded. "They told me the same. I contacted them because they filed a missing person's report two years ago."

"She's missing?" Tessa breathed, her heart skipping a beat at the thought. She hadn't known Anna well, but she'd liked her. As a matter of fact, she'd spent nearly a year trying to convince Anna's parents to let her visit.

"I'm afraid so. The last time they saw her was the three-year anniversary of the massacre."

"I don't like the way this is sounding," Seth said, his hand closing around Tessa's as if he could keep her safe by holding it.

Logan nodded and took another quick sip of coffee. "I thought the same when I heard about it."

"Do they have any idea what happened to her?" Tessa asked.

"She'd been suffering from depression after her injury, and her parents had been worried about her mental health. Her car was found near a river. The police assumed that she committed suicide, but her body was never found."

"So she could still be alive?" Seth said.

"It's a possibility. Of course, there's also the possibility that she didn't commit suicide and didn't disappear. That only leaves murder, and seeing as how Jack Dempsey was killed on the fourth anniversary of the massacre, I'm leaning toward that explanation." Logan eyed Tessa for a moment longer than was comfortable, his blue eyes sharp and hard.

"You don't think *I* killed her!" Tessa exclaimed, her heart thudding painfully.

"It never even crossed my mind. But I think you may know who did."

"I don't." Tessa jumped up. "If I did, don't you think I'd tell you?"

"Maybe not," Logan responded calmly. "Since you haven't been very forthcoming with information."

He was right, and she couldn't blame him for doubting her. "I apologize for that. I just…didn't know what to do. Besides, everyone I worked with in Kenya is dead. Even if they weren't, there's no one I can think of who'd commit murder."

"Not even Andrew?" Seth suggested.

She hesitated. Before the massacre, she'd have insisted that her brother-in-law wouldn't hurt a fly. Now, she wasn't so sure. "I don't know, but it doesn't matter. He's dead, too."

"Maybe," Logan intoned. "Or maybe he staged his death to cover his crimes. Maybe he used the massacre as a way to escape."

"No." Tessa shook her head, dizzy with the thought.

"It's okay, Tess." Seth slid an arm around her waist, urging her back into her chair, his hands resting on her shoulders.

"If he's alive, Tessa, would your brother-in-law have some reason to want to hurt you?" Logan asked.

"I don't think so, but how can I know? If he used the massacre to cover up his crimes, he's capable of anything, right?"

"Did you know what he was doing before the massacre?" he asked.

"No. I didn't even suspect it."

"When did you find out?"

"Not until afterward. Jack flew over, and he told me there'd been an investigation because mission funds were being misappropriated. All the evidence pointed to Andrew."

"There was irrefutable proof?"

"According to Jack, there was. He sent someone over to work with our team. She was there for a month before the massacre and was able to compile plenty of evidence."

"Do you know who it was?"

"I didn't while I was in Kenya, but Jack told me afterward that it was Anna."

Logan nodded, jotting notes in a small notepad. "Okay. That's a good start. I'm going to head to the office and make a few calls. Maybe someone from the mission board can clarify a few things for me. If you think of anything else that might be helpful, give me a call."

"I will. Thanks." Tessa followed Logan down the hall, holding the door open as he stepped into the late-morning sunlight.

Seth moved up behind her, his hands sliding around her waist and settling on her abdomen. "I need to leave, too. I have some paperwork to catch up on at the office," he said, his breath ruffling her hair and tickling her ear. "Will you be okay with just the patrol car out front?"

She nodded, but she didn't feel like she would be.

She felt as if she would fall apart if he let go of her, felt as if his arms were the only thing that stood between her and danger.

"Are you sure?" He nudged her around and looked into her eyes.

"I've been okay on my own for a long time. I think

I can manage." She tried to keep her tone light, tried to smile. The last thing she wanted was for him to spend his entire day worrying about her.

"Stay inside. Okay? No walking with Bentley. No answering the door unless you know exactly who it is. Don't go to work, to the grocery store or out on a drive, either."

"Anything else?" she asked wryly, but she was touched by his concern.

"Yes," he responded.

And then he leaned down and kissed her as if he meant it forever.

FIFTEEN

By four in the afternoon, Tessa was bored to tears.

Without work to take her mind off her troubles, and without a nice long run to perk her up, she felt draggy and morose.

She also felt like calling Seth. Just to check in, to see how his day was going.

To hear his voice.

She frowned. She should be more interested in calling Logan and finding out if he'd found evidence that his theory was correct and that Andrew was alive.

Just the thought made her shudder.

She'd spent five years believing that Andrew had paid the ultimate price for his crime. That had made keeping the secret more palatable.

But if he were alive, if he'd actually faked his death, then she'd been a fool.

She walked into her room, lifting the framed photo that she kept on her dresser. It was the only one she left out. She and Daniel on their wedding day. No sign of what would come. No huts or Kenyan villagers. Just the two of them standing in front of the little church they'd been married in.

She took it from the frame, running her finger along

a fold she'd made years ago and pulling it open. Andrew was to the left of Daniel, smiling into the camera.

She'd almost cut him out of the photo when she'd returned home from Kenya, but she hadn't had the heart. She'd still wanted to believe that he'd made a mistake, that he'd been greedy and thoughtless but without malice.

She was beginning to think that she'd been wrong.

She pulled her cell phone from the back pocket of her jeans and dialed Logan's number, leaving a voice mail message when he didn't pick up.

Outside, daylight was already fading, gray-blue dusk shadowing the landscape. A patrol car sat at the curb in front of the house. Tessa could see another at the corner of the street.

She should have felt safe.

She didn't.

She pulled the curtains closed, left the light on in her room, told herself twenty times that she shouldn't call Seth. He'd done enough for her. Too much, really. Sure, they'd shared a couple of kisses, but that didn't mean she should call him every time she wanted someone to talk to.

"Cookies are the answer," she announced to Bentley, and he opened an eye from his position near the fireplace, his tail thumping once on the floor. "You agree, right?"

He moaned, his eyes drifting closed.

So much for company while she baked.

She measured ingredients, following a recipe for white chocolate macadamia cookies that she'd learned during one of her foster placements. The wind picked up as she creamed butter and sugar together, the soft howl beneath the eaves sinister. She ignored it. She was jumpy. That was all. Too much talk about Kenya and the massacre.

And about Daniel and Andrew.

The only family she'd ever had.

That was why she hadn't wanted to believe the depth of Andrew's depravity. She sighed as she took out the finished cookies and slid the next pan in. The house smelled like sugar and vanilla, and her stomach rumbled. She ate a hot cookie, shaking her head as Bentley meandered into the room and sniffed the ground.

"Sorry, boy, I didn't even drop a crumb."

She reached for a second cookie as Bentley lifted his head and barked once, limping toward the front door.

Seconds later the doorbell rang.

Tessa hurried to the door, cookie in hand.

She glanced out the peephole, her heart doing a funny little jig as she looked into Seth's handsome face. "Hold on."

She unlocked the door and fumbled with the bolt, finally managing to slide it open.

"Hi," she said as she pulled the door open and stepped back to let him in.

Cool air swept in with him, carrying the fresh scent of the rain that had just begun to fall. She inhaled it, her heart racing as he closed the door.

He'd changed into black slacks and a button-down blue shirt, his black coat open to reveal his gun holster. One hand in his coat pocket, the other wrapped around a brown paper bag, he looked tough and unapproachable, but his smile left her breathless.

"Hi yourself. I finished my work early and thought that I'd stop by," he responded, his gaze dropping to the cookie she held. "You were baking."

"Yes. White chocolate macadamia."

"One of my favorites."

"Want one? I have a couple dozen that I shouldn't eat."

"Shouldn't or won't?" He took the cookie from her hand and bit into it, grinning when she frowned.

"Shouldn't. And that cookie was mine."

"You said you had a couple of dozen more. I figured you could spare this one." He finished it off, brushing crumbs from his coat. "Besides, I'm starving. I haven't eaten since this morning."

"I can make you something," she offered

"That would be nice," he said softly. "But I brought something for us to share." He held up brown paper bag.

Tessa caught a whiff of curry and hot peppers. "Chinese?"

"Thai."

"One of *my* favorites."

"Glad to hear it. Piper will be, too."

"Piper?" she asked as she led the way to the kitchen.

"My sister. It was her suggestion. She said you were a well-traveled woman and that you'd probably enjoy ethnic food."

"You called your sister to ask what I might like to eat for dinner?"

"She called me to see how my shoulder was doing. I decided to pick her brain and put her knowledge to good use." He smiled and set the bag on the kitchen table.

Her heart responded to his smile, her senses alive with the sight and scent of Seth. He filled her kitchen, and if she let him, he'd fill her life. She could feel it happening, feel the empty place in her heart filling up with him.

"Sit down. I'll get the plates." She turned her back

to him, standing on tiptoe and reaching for the plates on the top shelf of the cupboard.

"You're awfully short to be keeping things on shelves this high," Seth said mildly as he grabbed the plates for her, his chest pressing against her back.

"I'm not short, and the plates are up there because I never use them." She sidled out from between him and the counter, because being there was not good for her state of mind. When he was that close, she couldn't think straight.

"You don't eat at home?"

"Not big meals. It's not really worth my while to cook for one." She glanced at Bentley who hovered on the threshold of the kitchen. "And a half."

"A half? That dog is three of you." Seth pulled cartons from the bag and opened them, the spicy aroma that drifted out making Tessa's stomach growl.

"Thai basil chicken?" she asked as Seth spooned some onto each plate.

Seth nodded. "Another one of Piper's suggestions."

"Your sister is a smart lady."

"I'll tell her you said so when I see her."

"You're going for a visit?" she asked, the thought of Seth leaving town more upsetting than she wanted it to be. They weren't attached at the hip—he could do what he wanted when he wanted.

But she'd miss him.

"She's coming out here for Thanksgiving. My entire family is. Parents. Brothers. Sister. Spouses. Nieces and nephews. The whole shebang."

"That sounds like fun." She'd always loved the idea of a big family. She'd wanted at least four children, but Daniel had thought one or two would be plenty. He hadn't wanted anything to distract from his work and had insisted they wait at least five years before they considered adding to their family.

They hadn't made it to their fifth anniversary.

"It will be, and I was thinking—" he paused as he dug plastic utensils from the bag "—that their visit would be the perfect opportunity for all of you to meet."

"You want me to meet your family?" She knew she sounded shocked. Because she felt shocked.

"Sure. It's not often we're all together. If we wait until the next time it happens, it could be a year." Seth pulled out her chair and nudged her into it.

"Do you realize that we haven't even been on a date, and you're talking about me meeting your family?"

"I bought you Thai food, Tessa. Do you know how many miles I had to go to get it?"

"Seven."

He laughed. "Yes, and do you know how tempted I was to eat it all before I got here?"

"You're a saint, Seth, but that doesn't mean that this is a date or that I should meet your family."

"Maybe not, but you might as well know that I'm too old for games, and I'm not interested in taking things slow."

"Seth—"

"I wasn't looking for anyone, Tessa. Sometimes, though, we don't have to be looking to find what we need."

"What if it doesn't work out?" she asked quietly, her heart beating double time. "What if you only think you need me? What if—"

"Then we won't have lost anything for trying." He touched her hand, his palm warm against her skin.

Except our hearts, she wanted to add, but the food smelled wonderful, and Seth's eyes were the same blue as the evening sky, and it was easy to let the thought slip from her mind when he was looking at her like that.

Bentley nudged Seth's knee as he squeezed under the table and rested his head on Tessa's feet.

"You don't quite fit under there, big boy," Seth muttered, but he scratched Bentley's head and offered him a piece of chicken he plucked from a container of fried rice.

"You're not supposed to feed him table scraps," Tessa said, trying to sound firm. Seth could see right through her.

"I'm trying to win him over," he explained as he fed the big dog another piece of chicken. Truth be told, he was more interested in winning Tessa over. Now that he'd found her, he had no intention of letting her disappear from his life.

"Why would you want to do that?" she asked with a nervous laugh.

"I plan on spending a lot of time around here. Being buddies with your dog will make that easier. You don't mind, do you?" He looked into her eyes and wasn't surprised to see uncertainty. They'd both lost someone they'd deeply loved. They'd both been changed by it. It wasn't an easy thing to forget, and it wasn't easy to decide to move on.

He reached across the table and took her hand, sliding his thumb across her smooth skin. "I can leave if you want me to, Tessa. You can have the Thai food, no strings attached. Just a friend doing something for a friend."

"That isn't what this feels like," she said softly.

"I know, but if that's all that you want it to be, I'll be okay with that. No date. No meeting my family. No moving forward. I can do that if it's what you want."

"It isn't." Her fingers curved around his. "The thing is, I don't know how to do this."

"What?"

"You. Me. Us. Dinner." She swept her free hand in a circle that encompassed the table, the room and Seth. "Do you know how many years it's been since I've…"

"Dated?"

"That seems like a term for someone a lot younger than me."

"You're young."

"I don't feel young."

After a moment, he nodded in understanding. "Neither do I. We've both lived through a lot. We've survived—"

"So far," she offered with a sad smile.

"You'll be fine."

"We hope."

"*I* believe you're going to be fine, and I'm going to do everything in my power to make sure you are." He squeezed her hand gently. "So, how about we eat? We're letting our food get cold while we try to hash things out."

She hesitated, then nodded. "Okay."

It was a start, and it was enough.

Seth smiled. "Do you want to pray, or would you like me to?"

"You can." She bowed her head, and Seth offered a simple prayer of thanks for the food, resisting the urge to thank God for the company. The evening was young, the food smelled good and the company…

He looked into Tessa's eyes.

Perfect.

He didn't want to ruin that, didn't want to scare her by pushing too fast or too hard.

Tessa picked at her food, scooping up a few bites and then putting her fork down.

"I'm not as hungry as I thought I was," she announced, shoving her plate to the middle of the table. "I'm sorry."

"There's no need to apologize."

"I feel like there is. You're always doing so much for me, Seth." She grabbed the plate and covered it with plastic wrap. "It seems like the least I could do was enjoy it."

"If I didn't want to do things for you, I wouldn't. And when I do something for someone it isn't to get thanks or accolades." He grabbed a spring roll from a cardboard container.

"I know, but—"

"But nothing. Now, stop worrying or you'll make me lose my appetite," he cut her off.

She smiled, but her eyes were sad. "The way you're packing down that food, I'm not sure that's possible."

"Hey, it takes a lot of energy to do what I do."

"I thought you were on desk duty until your shoulder healed. You haven't been doing more than you're supposed to, have you?" She scowled, and Seth smiled.

"I'm glad to know you care, Tessa. No worries, though. I'm following the doctor's orders. I've just been burning the candle at both ends recently. That takes fuel. Which reminds me, I did a little digging while I was at work today," he said, and Tessa stiffened.

"Digging into what?"

"Your past." He'd wanted to find out more about Andrew and the mission team, and he'd pulled up old newspaper articles about the massacre. He'd been shocked to see Tessa's tearstained face on the front of several local newspapers. She'd looked like a kid, her hair in two long braids, her eyes large in her thin pale face. The story had taken center stage on the national news circuit. If Seth hadn't been on covert assignment overseas the year it had happened, there'd have been no way he wouldn't have known about it.

"I guess you're going to tell me what you found."

"You don't sound very happy about it."

"I'd be happy to never have to mention what happened in Kenya again." She walked to the window that looked out over the backyard. She'd pulled the shade, but he still wanted to drag her away, tell her that she had to be careful.

"Maybe one day you won't, but for right now—"

"I know, Seth. I'm going to have to discuss it. I'm going to have to answer questions. I'm going to have to relive every bit of the horror." She turned to face him again, her eyes the same misty green as Smith Mountain Lake in the morning. Looking into them was like looking into the past, like seeing the future, like returning home after too many years away.

He covered the space between them in two short steps and took both her hands in his. "If you'd rather not, it can wait, Tess. I can give the information to Logan and let him use it."

"It can't wait. Not really. Not if I want to stay alive, and I do. What did you find?"

"An interview that Anna did about a year after the massacre. It was for a local paper, and she was talking about how God had saved her. She hinted that the mission team had gotten what it deserved. Said that she'd survived because her focus had been on helping the Kenyan people rather than making her name or building her wealth."

Tessa stilled, her muscles tensing. "You think she knew about Andrew."

"I don't know, and she's not around to question. Do you remember what she was like?"

"Sweet. Very committed to serving God. I can't imagine her hurting anyone."

"Tragedy changes people. It's possible it made her bitter. Maybe even made her want revenge"

"It sure changed me." She sighed. "But we don't even know if Anna is alive. As a matter of fact, we don't really know much of anything."

"We know that someone connected to your time in Kenya is in the States, and we know that whoever it is, is coming after you. I won't be satisfied until that person is behind bars."

"I'll be okay. Isn't that what you're always saying to me?" Her hands rested on his waist, tentative and light, her smile sweet. She smelled like sunshine and flowers, her skin soft as a rose petal as he touched her bare arms.

"Have I told you lately how beautiful you are with flour in your hair?" he asked.

"I have flour—"

"Just here." He gently brushed the dusting of white from the fiery hair near her temple. "Of course, you're always beautiful."

"Seth, I—"

"How about we not discuss all the reasons why this isn't a good idea, and spend a little time talking about why it is?" He cupped her shoulders, studying her face—her fair skin and dusting of freckles; her golden-red lashes and strong cheekbones. It wasn't her beauty that tempted him, though. It was her. Everything about Tessa appealed to him, and he thought that if he lived another hundred years, he wouldn't meet a woman who filled his thoughts the way that she did.

"What if I'm not ready for a relationship?" she asked, her voice soft.

"Then I'll wait until you are, and we'll go from there," he responded honestly. She rewarded him with a wry smile.

"You're too good to be true."

"Try telling my siblings that. They'll set you straight."

"At your big Thanksgiving get-together?"

"If you want."

She stared into his eyes for a moment. Finally, she nodded. "I think I do," she whispered.

"Great. Hopefully, being around them won't convince you that I'm less than the perfect specimen of humanity that you obviously think I am," he teased.

"Never." Tessa laughed, stretching up on her toes and pressing a quick kiss to his cheek.

He turned his head, capturing her lips with his, and just like that he was lost in her, lost in the way it felt to be so close to her.

When his cell phone rang, it took him a minute to hear it, and he had trouble breaking away. "Sinclair here."

"It's Logan. One of my officers just reported movement on the hill above Tessa's house."

"What kind of movement?" Seth walked to the window above the sink, slowly pulled the shade aside and looked out into the backyard. A small light jumped through the woods near the top of the ridge.

"A light. It's been there and gone a few times over the past hour. It looks like whoever it is is moving closer. I've dispatched officers to check it out."

"I'm going to check it out, too." He glanced at Tessa.

She looked scared. Good. As long as she was scared, she'd play it safe, stay close to home and make it easier for the people who were trying to help her succeed. "You have an officer stationed outside her house, right?"

"Yes, but—"

"As long as Tessa is locked in, and your man is doing his job, she'll be fine. The more people we have up on that hill, the more likely it will be that we'll find the guy who's after her." He disconnected, shoved the phone in his pocket and grabbed his coat.

"What's going on?" Tessa asked as she followed him to the back door.

"Someone is up on the hill behind your house."

"People walk there all the time."

"With flashlights?"

She paused. "Not that I've ever noticed."

"That's what I figured. Logan already has an officer out searching. I'm going, too. You need to stay near the front of the house. Keep the doors locked and don't go near the windows."

"Maybe you should leave it to the police." She bit her lower lip.

"I'll be fine." He leaned over and gave her a quick kiss, the warmth of her lips making him want to stay by her side. He forced himself to move away from her and stepped out onto the back deck. "Lock the door. I'll be back as soon as I can."

He ran across the dark yard, his feet crunching the nearly frozen grass. The night seemed too still, too quiet, the air heavy with rain and the dark energy that seemed to precede trouble.

The hair on the back of his neck stood on end, his body humming with adrenalin.

He glanced up the hill, and saw the light bob once

and then go out. He dove behind a small shrub near the edge of the property. Someone *had* been watching the house. Whoever it was had seen him walk out the back door.

Did the person have a handgun or rifle?

Did he have night-vision goggles?

The questions shot through his mind as he eased along the property line and stepped into the deep shadows at the base of the hill.

Please, God, help me find him. Please keep Tessa safe.

He continued to pray silently for the woman he was falling in love with as he slowly made his way deeper into the forest.

SIXTEEN

Tessa knew exactly what she was supposed to do.

Stay near the front of the house.

With two police cars parked on her street there was little chance that someone was going to take a shot at her from that direction.

The woods behind her house were a different story. They were so dense that it would be fairly easy for someone to hide there during the day. At night, a person would be almost impossible to spot. If an attack were going to come, it would come from that direction.

But even though she needed to stay near the front, she wanted to go look out back. That's the way Seth had gone, and she had the absurd urge to go after him, to drag him back to the safety of the house.

She walked into the living room, pacing near the fireplace.

Seth was risking his life for her.

It didn't feel good.

It felt even worse to cower in the house while he did it.

"Please, Lord, keep him safe," she prayed aloud, because she didn't know what else to do. She wanted desperately to believe that He was there, ready and willing to help.

Bentley whined in response, his tail brushing the living room floor. If she let him out back, he'd probably take off in whatever direction Seth had gone. More than likely, he'd make enough noise to scare any bad guys away.

Or to get himself shot again.

She frowned, crouching next to the big dog and scratching his knobby head. "I wouldn't want you to get hurt again, Bentley. You're going to have to stay close to home for a while. As a matter of fact, I want you to stay right here. Stay!"

He barked, licked her hand and sat at attention, waiting for her next command.

Good. One problem solved.

Tessa turned off the living room light and the light in the hall, making sure there was no way she'd be backlit when she went into the kitchen. Then she crept through the dining room, crouching low as she passed the windows.

Bentley barked, the sound so startling that Tessa jumped.

She glanced back and saw that he was inching toward her on his belly.

"I said *stay*," she commanded, and he sat near the dining room doorway, even though she could tell he didn't like doing it one bit.

Hopefully, he'd stay there.

The house fell silent again as she inched her way to the sink and looked out the window. Nothing moved in the yard. Not even the leaves on the trees near the edge of the lawn. The forest stretched black and thick along the hill. Whatever light Seth had seen was gone. Hopefully, whoever had been carrying the light was gone, too.

Please, Lord, please keep him safe, she prayed as she scanned the ridge at the top of the hill. She'd walked there dozens of times during the day. She'd always felt safe—the trail that led through the woods was well traveled by people in the community. She'd been on it after dark only a few times. Things were different then, of course. What was safe during the day often seemed dangerous when the sun went down.

She felt that as she stared up the hill. A million eyes could be staring back, and she wouldn't know it. She shivered, but didn't go back to the living room.

Seth had gone to hunt for the person who was hunting her. She didn't take that lightly. Everything he'd said about dating and meeting his family and moving forward to see where they were heading would mean nothing if he died. And if he did, it would be because of her.

Please.

She prayed again, wondering if God were listening. If He cared. She'd often wondered where He'd been when Daniel was murdered. She'd wondered if He'd heard when children and their mothers were screaming for mercy. A piece of her soul had rebelled at the idea of God allowing such carnage. She'd believed in His mercy, His love, even His judgment, but she'd never believed Him to be cruel. Seeing the bodies lying between the huts, holding Daniel bleeding body while he whispered for her to go and not look back, living through the horror of all those things had made her wonder if God had turned His back and didn't care enough to intervene.

Her faith had been shaken, but then, she wasn't sure how strong it had been to begin with.

She'd wanted it to be strong, because Daniel had always been so certain and committed. His zeal had been infectious, and she had to admit that he had carried the weight of their faith. She'd allowed it because it had been more comfortable than searching her heart and finding out how hollow her own faith was.

While Daniel had asked for God's will to be revealed, Tessa had simply asked that He reveal Himself to her.

Are You there? That's what she'd wanted to ask more often than not. If Daniel had suspected her spiritual failure, he'd never let on. They'd prayed together, worshiped together, put their lives in God's hands together.

But, Tessa's faith had been a dim reflection of Daniel's, and when she'd needed it most, she hadn't been able to find it. She hadn't felt God's presence that night of the massacre, but maybe her shock and horror blinded her to it. Her eyes burned at the thought, her throat tight and hot. She'd spent five years feeling alone, running from one town to another to avoid the past and all its troubles. Was it possible that God had been directing her every step? That He truly had intended for her to end up exactly where she was—in Pine Bluff, Washington, with Seth Sinclair?

Being with Seth seemed right when so many other things in her life hadn't.

That had to mean something.

Didn't it?

She sighed and paced through the living room, looking out the front window. The police car was still parked at the curb. She waved, but couldn't quite see the officer through the darkness.

She wanted to go outside and ask if he'd heard anything about the person on the hill. But she doubted he'd appreciate her questions, and he'd probably be un-

happy to have her walking across the yard when someone could be skulking in the gloom.

A year ago, she would have packed her bags and run,
found a new house in a new town, tried to forget that
trouble was following her. She wouldn't do that this
time. She loved Pine Bluff. She loved her house and job.

And Seth…

They had plans. Together.

Thanksgiving with his family.

She had spent one too many holidays alone. Five
years' worth of holidays that had echoed the silence
and emptiness of her life.

Last year, she'd spent Thanksgiving serving food at
a homeless shelter. She'd needed to remind herself how
blessed and fortunate she was to have a house, food,
clothes. She'd needed to make sure that she didn't dwell
in the self-pity that seemed to rear its ugly head during
holiday seasons.

This year, she could have something different. She
could be part of a family celebration. She clenched her
fists, worried about just how much she wanted that. It
scared her to think of how vulnerable it made her, how
easily she could be hurt if she wasn't careful.

She settled onto the rocking chair, wishing she had
the guts to walk into the mudroom and grab a couple
of pieces of wood for the fireplace. A little warmth and
light wouldn't be a bad thing. The wind picked up, rat-
tling the windows and blowing icy rain against the glass.
Seth was out in this mess, struggling through the forest
with an injured shoulder—for her.

While she sat like a lump and waited.

She fingered her cell phone, wanting desperately to
call him, to make sure he was okay. But she was afraid

that if she did, she'd somehow thrust him into worse danger.

The wind rattled the window again, and she jumped up.

No way could she keep sitting and waiting—she had to do something.

She grabbed her coat and wrapped a scarf around her neck.

"Stay," she ordered Bentley as he jumped up to follow her. She walked to the back door, yanked it open and nearly barreled into Seth's hard chest. He grabbed her arms, holding her steady as he walked her backward into the mudroom. He closed the door and locked it.

"What in the world are you doing?" He pulled her into the living room, his eyes such a dark blue they were almost black.

"I was worried. You're walking around in the middle of a storm with a bad shoulder, and—"

"My shoulder is fine. My temper, on the other hand, is getting the better of me," he growled. "How do you think I'd have felt if I got back and you were gone— or worse?" He looked tired, his eyes deeply shadowed, and Tessa's heart responded, opening to him in a way she hadn't expected it could.

"I'm sorry. I just couldn't sit still, thinking of you out there in danger because of me." She wrapped her arms around his waist and lay her head against his chest. She could hear the rapid beat of his heart, feel its solid thud beneath her ear.

She wanted to cry. For everything she missed, for all the things she thought she'd never have again, for what she just might find in the safety of Seth's arms.

She felt his anger give way as he put his arms around

her. "Don't ever do something like that again," he said gruffly.

"I won't."

"Even if you're worried?" He slid his hands inside her coat, his palms resting against her back.

"I'm not going to make any promises."

"Tess—"

"Did you find anything in the woods?" She cut him off, because she didn't want to ruin the moment with an argument.

He frowned but switched gears. "I followed the light up to the service road and heard a car driving away. Unfortunately, I didn't get a look at it."

"Maybe Logan—"

"His men came up empty, too. He's calling in a search-and-rescue dog, hoping to pick up a scent, but unless we find something that belongs to the perpetrator, that will be tough to do."

"Too bad. I was hoping that this nightmare was finally going to end."

"I know, and it will. Soon." He dropped a quick kiss on her forehead. "Until it does, Logan is going to keep several patrol cars stationed on your street. There's an officer out back, too. You'll be safe as long as you stay inside."

"Are you leaving?"

"I wish I didn't have to," he frowned, his finger skimming along the tender flesh beneath her eyes. "But, you're exhausted, and I have work to do."

"What kind of work?"

"I want to see what else I can find out about your brother-in-law."

"You really think there's a chance that he's alive, don't you?"

"Yes, and if he is, he's the person we're looking for. Stay safe, okay?" He kissed her tenderly, and walked outside, closing the door and leaving her there, his kiss still warm on her lips.

Tessa sighed and flicked off the foyer light, whistled for Bentley and went into her room. She kept the light off as she changed into flannel pajamas and dropped onto the bed. The hallway light shone under the door, casting the room in shades of gray and black. It was early, but she was exhausted, her brain foggy from too many sleepless nights. Bentley lumbered up beside her, circled around and finally settled down, his heavy body taking up half the bed. She didn't have the heart to nudge him away. Besides, it felt good to have her friend back.

She closed her eyes, thought about the light Seth had seen on the hill behind her house and opened them again.

Someone was stalking her, biding his time, waiting for the right opportunity to finish what he'd started.

Could it really be Andrew?

Seth seemed to think so.

What if he was right? What if Andrew really were alive? Maybe he'd just been biding his time, waiting for an opportunity to get rid of some loose ends. Jack. Anna. *Tessa.*

Was it truly possible that her own brother-in-law— the brother of the man she had dedicated her life to— was coming for her because of what she knew?

Of course it was.

If Andrew had been willing to use children to do his dirty work in Kenya, there probably wasn't much he wouldn't do. Including killing her.

She frowned, turning on her side, Bentley moaning as she jostled him.

She pulled the covers up a little higher, listening to the silent house and wishing that she was still standing in her kitchen, safe in Seth's arms.

SEVENTEEN

Tessa woke to the sound of howling wind and ice splattering against the roof. The house lay still and silent. No light from the hallway shining in under the door.

No hum of the heater.

Nothing.

She pushed aside the blanket, shivering in the frigid air, realizing that Bentley was no longer next to her. She looked to see what time it was. The alarm clock was out. No glowing lights to tell her whether it was night or morning. Had the electricity had been knocked out by the storm?

If it hadn't...

She wasn't going there. There was no sense panicking until she was sure there was something to panic about. She stood, calling for Bentley, and was relieved to hear him pad across the floor.

He bumped his nose against her hand, and she scratched his head. If he wasn't barking, everything was fine. That should have been comforting, but she still felt uneasy, her heart beating just a little too quickly. She glanced at her cell phone display. Three-thirty. Not even close to dawn. Was Seth awake? Still working on investigating Andrew?

She thought about calling, but what would she say? That the electricity had gone out, and she was wide awake? Bored, scared and lonely?

No. She wasn't going to disturb him over something so silly. Especially not when there were police officers outside, guarding the house.

But, she *was* wide-awake now and sure that she wouldn't be able to get back to sleep. Too bad. She'd rather sleep through the power outage and wake up when the sun was up. At least then she wouldn't be imagining danger lurking in every shadow of the room.

"What do you think, boy?" She scratched Bentley's head again, more to comfort herself than to please him. "Should we go downstairs and make some tea? Maybe start a fire?"

Bentley whined impatiently, and she opened the door, letting him precede her into the hallway. The darkness was almost complete, just hints of gray light spilling in through the windows on either side of the front door. The kitchen was silvery black, the old wood floor creaking as Tessa flicked on the gas burner and set the teakettle to boil.

She grabbed candles from a cupboard above the refrigerator, lit them and set them on the counter. A little light always made things less scary.

She walked into the mudroom, grabbed newspaper from the recycling bin and two logs from the stack near the door. She carried everything back to the fireplace. A few crumbled up sheets of newspaper and a quick flash of the match, and the flames shot up, greedily eating at the dry wood. Bentley settled down on the bed she'd made him.

The teakettle whistled, the sound mournful and haunting against the backdrop of the storm and crackling fire. Tessa hurried into the kitchen and turned off the burner, poured boiling water over a tea bag and carried the mug into the living room.

She sat in the old rocking chair just as Bentley shifted, then stood, growling low in his throat as he stared at the front window. The hair on the back of her neck stood on end, and Tessa crept toward the window, her hand shaking as she pulled back the heavy fabric.

She didn't know what she expected to see. A face? A gun? She saw nothing but the icy yard. Beyond it, the road glittered, the police cruiser parked at the curb, spitting white exhaust into the darkness. A truck was parked in the field across from it, headlights off, the gleaming hood of the vehicle the only hint that it was there.

Seth's truck?

She thought so, but the storm and the darkness made it difficult to be certain.

She wanted to be certain, though, because if Seth was out in his truck, he may as well join her in the house.

She reached for her cell phone but Bentley barked. She dropped the curtain and jumped back.

"What's going on, Bentley?" she asked, her voice shaking.

He padded to the front door and barked again as the doorbell rang.

Someone banged on the door, and Tessa's heart jumped. She screamed, and then clapped a hand over her mouth, willing herself to be quiet as terror took over and she froze.

"Tessa?" Seth called through the heavy wooden door. He was ready to break it down if he had to, her muffled scream still echoing in his ears. He'd seen the light of a fire flickering through a crack in the living room curtain, and he'd known she was awake. He'd assumed she was safe, the house locked up tight.

Now, he wasn't so sure.

"Hold on," she responded.

The lock turned, the bolt sliding open.

Seconds later, Tessa peered out through the crack in the door. "What in the world are you doing out there?"

"Checking on you." He gave the door a gentle push, and she let it open wider. "You screamed."

"After you rang the doorbell and nearly scared me to death." She sounded both shaky and relieved, her face parchment pale in the dark foyer.

"I saw that you'd lit a fire. I figured you were awake. It stood to reason that if we were both awake, we may as well be awake together."

"You're not supposed to be awake in your truck outside my house. You're supposed to be home. Researching Andrew or sleeping."

"I *was* home. Changed my clothes and came back to stake out the house. I wanted to keep an eye on the hill. See if our guy showed up again."

"You can't guard me twenty-four hours a day. It's not practical." Even in the darkness, he could see the circles beneath her eyes and the tension in her face.

"I'm not worried about practical. I'm worried about you." He pulled her into his arms, smiling as her hands slid around his waist and rested on his back. It felt so natural, so right for her to respond to him this way. "What are you doing awake at three in the morning?"

"The electricity went out. The quiet woke me," she mumbled against his chest.

"So how about we sit by that fire you made? Maybe that'll make you sleepy again." He sat on the sofa, pulling her down next to him. "You're a regular Girl Scout, Tessa. The fire looks great."

"I was never a Girl Scout."

"Never a Scout? I thought that was a prerequisite for every girl and boy when we were kids." He pressed her head to his shoulder, running his hand through her silky hair.

"My parents were too busy partying to take me to meetings. After they died, I was in foster care, and the families I was in had way too many kids to worry about things like Girl Scouts."

"I'm sorry, Tessa." He couldn't imagine what it was like to grow up without a family who cared, to not have that support system, that safety net.

"There are worse things a kid can miss out on, Seth. Scouting isn't that important."

"I'm not talking about scouting. I'm talking about family. Love. The things every kid deserves."

"You still don't need to be sorry. I survived, and I turned out just fine."

"Better than fine," he said, and she laughed softly, her body heavy against his, her warmth seeping through his coat. He'd wanted to share a moment like this with her as much as he'd wanted anything in a long time, but he didn't speak. He just watched the firelight flicker across her fair skin. She deserved so much more than what she'd been given in life. He wanted to make sure she got it. He kept the thought to himself, not wanting to chase her away.

The moment was too nice.

The fire too perfect.

And, Tess… She was just about perfect, too.

She shifted, sitting up so that she could look him in the eye. "You're too good to be true, you know that, Seth?"

"I'm not good, Tessa. I'm just me."

"And I'm me, and that makes me cautious." She pulled her knees up to her chest, wrapping her arms around them. "When I met Daniel, I was desperate for a family. I'd been in foster care for eight years, and I wanted someone to love me. He did."

"You don't have to talk about this, Tessa."

"I want to, because it explains who I am. Why I can't just believe that everything is going to work out the way I hope." She shrugged, her hair sliding like red silk around her shoulders. "Daniel and I were good friends. We loved each other. I thought we'd have forever together. The thing is, I accepted Andrew because of Daniel. I wanted to believe that we would be the big happy family I'd always wanted."

"You can't blame yourself for not seeing through Andrew's lies."

"Sure I can. Andrew and I were never close. He and Daniel got along great, though. *They* were really close. When they were kids, they did everything together," she said, her words wistful. "But Daniel told me stories about Andrew. About how he'd gotten into trouble when they were kids."

"What kind of trouble?"

"He shoplifted a couple of times when he was in high school and got caught. Once, he stole a car. The way Daniel and his parents told it, he was a typical kid and kids make mistakes."

"Those are some pretty big mistakes."

"I thought the same, but I never saw any sign that he was planning to go back to…" Her voice trailed off, and Seth thought that if the light was better, he'd see her cheeks flush.

"His life of crime?" he offered.

"If that's what you want to call it."

"What else is there? Sure, kids get into trouble, but most kids aren't arrested several times before they turn eighteen."

"I know," Tessa reluctantly agreed. She'd often thought exactly what Seth was saying, but she'd loved Daniel's family too much to ever imply that Andrew's behavior was anything other than childish indiscretion. "But he never got in trouble after he turned eighteen. I don't even think he'd had a parking ticket. His parents said that he'd finally grown into himself. They were so proud of him," she whispered, not sure if she was speaking to Seth or to herself.

"I'm sure your husband was, too."

She nodded, because she couldn't speak past the lump in her throat. Had she blinded herself so much that she'd refused to see the signs? Had the rest of the family?

"Tessa, there's no way you could have known what would happen. No one could have," Seth said quietly.

"You told me that before, but how can I know that for sure? Maybe I wanted so badly to be part of Daniel's family that I overlooked signs that could have saved lives."

"What signs?" Seth prodded.

She'd wondered that hundreds of times in the years since the massacre. "Andrew always seemed a little reserved. He was never as open and easygoing as Daniel."

"Plenty of people are reserved without being criminals."

"I know, but maybe if I'd—"

"Don't." Seth tugged her into his arms. "It's easy to look back and see what we think might have been there. That doesn't mean it *was* there."

"What if I'm looking back and seeing what *was* there? What if it all could have been prevented? What if—"

"What if you stop looking back, Tessa?"

Seth was staring at her, looking deep into her eyes. She saw so much in his gaze. So many things she thought she'd never see again.

His question hung in the air.

"I can't. Not until this is over." She stood, moving away from Seth and the promises she saw in his eyes.

"This will be over eventually. You know that, right?" He moved up beside her, close but not touching. She was acutely aware of him—every breath, every movement.

"It's been going on for five years. Who's to say that it won't continue for another five?"

"Me. I'm not going to let the creep who's after you continue the game he's playing," Seth retorted.

"You mean Andrew, right? That's who you really think it is."

"It would make sense. But, even if it's not, we're going to find the guy responsible, and we're going to stop him."

"You have a lot more confidence than I do." She pulled back the curtain and looked out into the front yard. The police cruiser still sat at the curb. "Maybe I should just hide somewhere until the guy is caught. Just go away and pretend that I'm someone else. You could help me do that, Seth. I know you've probably helped dozens of people change their identities."

Seth laughed, the sound rough and warm all at the same time. It sank into her heart and seemed to want to stay there.

"What's so funny?" she snapped, irritated with her

heart's response, irritated with him because he just seemed so...perfect.

"I'm a personal security specialist, Tessa. Not a federal marshal. I protect people. I don't help them disappear."

"It's not that funny." But Tessa smiled.

"You should do that more often." He traced the curve of her lips. "You're breathtaking when you smile."

She wanted to lean in, wanted to believe that he was everything she'd hoped and prayed for when she was a lonely teenager. Everything she needed to fill the emptiness that had been in her heart for too long.

"And you're a temptation that I'm finding difficult to resist," she replied with a sigh.

He smiled gently, his fingers lacing with hers. "Why should you?"

"Because I don't want to lose everything again. I don't think I could survive it this time."

"God brought us into each other's lives for a reason, Tessa. I don't think it was so that we could walk out of them again."

She wanted to tell him that God could have had dozens of reasons for bringing them together, but when she looked into his eyes, she could think only of how wonderful it would be if he were right. "I hope you're right, Seth. I really do."

"Don't hope, honey. Believe," he whispered against her hair. "Because when God is in it, everything works out just the way it should."

As she stood in his arms and looked out into the dawning day, she began to believe that he was exactly right.

EIGHTEEN

"Three days stuck in this house is two days too many, Bentley," Tessa griped as she dry mopped the floor for what felt like the hundredth time. When she was busy working, she didn't worry about dust bunnies and dirty throw rugs. When she wasn't, it was a different story.

She shook her head, lifting the throw rug from in front of the fireplace. Just standing there was enough to make her blush, the memory of Seth's eyes, his lips, his sweet promises, making her want to pick up the phone and call him.

She didn't want to be too needy, though. She didn't want him to think she'd be one of the kind who always needed to know where her man was.

Her man?

"Is that what he is?" she asked the dog. He snuffled the rug and settled down next to the fireplace.

"You need to be a better conversationalist, Bentley."

Bentley ignored her, and she carried the rug to the back door and hesitated. It was full light, nearly eight in the morning, and she couldn't imagine danger lurking out in her backyard.

Just because she couldn't imagine it didn't mean it wasn't there. Seth had warned her dozens of times over the past few days. Though Logan had been burning candles at both ends trying to find out if Andrew's body had ever been properly identified, he hadn't been successful. He hadn't been able to find Anna, either, and he'd conceded that both could be dead, and that the person stalking Tessa could be someone unrelated to Kenya.

Tessa didn't think he believed it, though, and she knew that Seth didn't, either. Like the deputy sheriff, he'd dedicated most of the past three days to the investigation. Just like the sheriff's department, he'd come up empty.

She frowned and dropped the throw rug on the floor near the back door. It could wait until… She wasn't sure how long it would have to wait, how many more days or weeks she'd be cloistered in her house. Too many more, and she'd go stir crazy.

The phone rang, and she rushed to answer it, anxious for the distraction. "Hello?"

"Tessa? It's Seth," Seth said, as if he needed an introduction, as if she hadn't recognized his voice the moment he'd said her name. Her hand tightened on the phone, and she sat in a kitchen chair, smiling because it was him and just talking to him made her feel happier.

"What's up? It's a little early for a phone call, isn't it?"

"Were you sleeping?"

"I was up before dawn. I was just thinking about taking a nap."

"I'd think you were more likely to be cleaning something. The floors, maybe?"

"How did you know?" She laughed, her cheeks heating as his warm chuckle drifted across the line.

"My keen powers of deduction and the fact that I'm

parked outside and could see you through the front window."

"How long have you been out there?" she asked, moving to the living room window, her heart leaping as she saw Seth's truck parked behind the police cruiser.

"Just long enough to see you put down the broom and pick up the throw rug." He got out of the car, his hair gleaming in the morning sunlight. He looked good. So good, she almost opened the door and ran into his arms. "You weren't planning to bring the rug out back, were you?" he continued, his words pulling her away from her thoughts.

"I considered it." She opened the front door, still holding the phone to her ear, her heart beating wildly as Seth made his way up the porch stairs.

There was just something about him.

Something that made every nerve respond, every thought spin back toward him.

"Think we can hang up now?" He held up the phone and smiled.

"It makes more sense than talking on the phone while we're standing next to each other," Tessa replied.

"You know what makes even more sense?" He took both her hands, urging her backward into the house. "This."

One kiss, and she was lost, the past gone. Just her and Seth and nothing to worry about but the next breath they'd take, the next moment they'd share.

Seth broke away. "You'd better go get dressed. It's going to be a busy day." He leaned down to scratch Bentley's head.

"I am dressed." Maybe not all that well, but her worn jeans and faded sweater had seemed perfect for cleaning the house. Of course, if she'd known Seth was com-

ing for an early morning visit, she'd have chosen jeans
that fit a little better and a shirt she'd had for less than
four years.

"I think you've forgotten what day it is," he chided,
tugging at a sapphire-blue tie that he'd paired with a
striped shirt.

"I guess I have."

"Sunday, Tessa." He hooked a strand of her hair behind her ear. "I thought we'd go to church together. Get
some lunch afterward. Then we need to head over to
the sheriff's department. Logan finally heard from the
police in Kenya."

Tessa stiffened at his words, and Seth wished he'd
waited to tell her. She'd been on edge the past few days,
and the dark circles under her eyes spoke of sleepless
nights and too much worry.

"What did they say?" she asked, her tone as stiff as
her muscles.

"Not much. They faxed him their report, and he
wants to go over it with us. He would have called you
but I checked in with him this morning, and he asked
me to give you the message. He'll come here if you
want him to."

"I...don't know if I can talk about the details of what
happened. It's been five years, but it seems like yes-
terday." She dropped onto the couch, her shoulders
slumped, her face pale and drawn.

"You're way stronger than you give yourself credit
for, Tessa." He didn't sit, because if he did, he'd reach
for her. And once she was in his arms, everything that
he wanted to say—everything that she needed to say—
would be lost.

"You give me a lot more credit than you should." She

sighed and stood. "But you're right. I can't avoid it, and I do need to go to church. And eat."

"And spend time with a good looking ex-soldier?" He was rewarded with a half smile.

"That, too. Give me twenty minutes." She headed up the stairs looking exhausted, and he almost felt bad for interrupting her quiet morning.

The fact was, he hadn't slept much lately, either. He'd spent most of the past few nights digging into Andrew Camry's past, calling his old friends and enemies, reading a few newspaper articles that had been written before the mission trip. There was no record of Andrew's crimes, but people who'd known him when he was a kid had been willing to talk. The stories they'd told weren't good ones. He'd been a bully, a thief and a liar. Most people believed that had changed in the years before he went to Kenya, but a few insisted that Andrew had been a bad apple. Rotten to the core, one had said.

It was hard to know the truth of the matter.

Especially with Andrew dead.

Or not.

Kenyan police and the U.S. consulate had spent two years searching for his body. Eventually, they'd been led to a partial skeleton buried near the village Andrew had been taken from. But no one could say for sure whether the bones had been Andrew's—no DNA testing had been done, because aside from Tessa, there'd been no family to claim the body, no one who cared enough to find out for sure whether or not the bones belonged to him.

"I'm ready," Tessa called from the top of the steps, and Seth looked up, his pulse racing as she walked toward him.

She was beautiful, her hair straight and silky, swinging around her shoulders. She'd traded her jeans and sweater for a long-sleeved gray dress that complemented her slender figure. He'd never seen her in makeup but she wore subtle hints of it now, accenting her lovely features.

"You're stunning," he breathed, taking her hand as she stepped off the last step.

"You're not so bad yourself," she responded, the color in her cheeks deepening.

He kissed her gently, his hand still curved around hers.

He'd met and fallen in love with Julia when he was a kid, and he hadn't fallen in love with anyone since then. He hadn't intended to have that kind of relationship with anyone else—he'd only wanted the kind of light and easy bond that didn't hurt when it was broken.

But he'd stumbled into Tessa's life, fallen into the green depths of her eyes. He wouldn't change that even if he could.

"I guess we'd better get out of here." She pulled back, her lips deep pink from his kiss, her cheeks flushed. "We don't want to be late for church."

"True, but I wouldn't mind spending a little more time here with you," he murmured as he helped her into her coat and started buttoning it.

She brushed his hands away. "I'm not a child, Seth."

"Trust me, I'm very aware of that," he responded dryly.

Her blush deepened and she turned away, tugging the thick fall of her hair from her collar. "What do you think Logan wants to discuss? Just the report? Or do you think he found something in it?"

"He didn't say." He opened the front door, letting cold fall air into the foyer. He'd grown up where the weather was still mild in November, but in Washington, winter seemed to take hold before October ended, the air growing cold, the sky gray.

"You asked, though, didn't you?" She edged in close.

"I asked. He said he wanted to discuss it with you. I told him we'd be in to speak to him after church." Logan hadn't been happy about that, but Seth hadn't cared. Fear and tension were taking their toll on Tessa, and she needed a break from the stress.

"We could go now," she said, apparently as eager for the meeting as Logan.

"You need a break, Tess. Some time away from the house and away from the investigation. At least, I thought you did. If I was wrong—"

"You weren't," she admitted, offering him a small smile. "A few hours not focusing on my troubles would be…nice."

"Let's get to it, then." He glanced at the officer who sat in a cruiser at the curb in front of Tessa's house. The guy nodded and gave a quick salute. Up the street, another cruiser sat, engine running, exhaust puffing out. Everything looked clear, the morning quiet and still, but Seth hesitated, a warning whispering at the back of his mind.

"What's wrong?" Tessa whispered, her arm pressed against his, her muscles taut.

"Probably nothing," he responded, shifting so that he completely blocked her view of the street.

"Then why are you trying to keep me from seeing what's outside?"

"Just being cautious."

And paranoid? Seth wanted to think that lack of sleep was making him imagine threats where there weren't any, but he'd spent most of his life listening to his gut.

"Tell you what. Go sit down in the living room. I want to check the perimeter of the house before we head out."

"You think someone is out there," she accused.

He couldn't deny it, so he walked her to the couch, gave her a gentle nudge. "Sit here. I'll be back in a minute."

"I thought we agreed that neither of us were good at taking orders," she muttered, but she sat.

Good.

He wanted to check things out, and he didn't want to be worrying about Tessa while he did it.

"When it comes to you, I'm not all that fond of giving them, but I want you safe, so stay put." He tossed the warning over his shoulder as he walked outside.

Bright sunlight gleamed off the roof of the patrol car as Seth approached it. The officer rolled down the window, eying him through dark sunglasses. "Everything okay?"

"I came out to ask you the same thing."

"It's been quiet since I got here at seven. The guy I replaced said the same thing." The officer pushed his sunglasses up and frowned. "Why? Did you hear or see something?"

"No." Seth scanned the road. "But it isn't what I can hear and see that has me worried."

"Like I said, it's been quiet as a tomb out here. If anything changes, I'll let you know."

"We're planning to head to church. You want to follow?" An extra set of eyes and an extra weapon were always good, and Seth had never been above asking for help when he thought he might need it.

"Sure." The officer pushed his glasses back into place and rolled up the window. Nothing changed. No sudden movement from across the street. No crackle of underbrush near the edge of the yard. No more reason to be on guard than Seth had had before, but he felt even more on edge as he searched the perimeter of the property.

Nothing.

He stared at the hill behind the house, searching the thick trees for any sign that someone was there. Movement, a shift in branches, something.

The hill was as quiet and still as the morning. Too quiet and too still in Seth's opinion, but he had nothing to pin the thought on.

He walked back to the house, pausing on the porch and scanning the front yard again.

"See anything?" Tessa asked through the door.

He turned. She'd cracked the door open and was looking out at him. "No."

"So," she said as she opened the door, "I guess we can leave."

"Right."

"Then why aren't we going?" She walked out onto the porch, and Seth stepped between her and the street.

"We are." He led her to his truck, ushering her in as quickly as he could. This early on a Sunday morning, it wasn't surprising that Tessa's neighborhood was quiet, but he couldn't shake the concern that nudged at the back of his mind as he slid behind the wheel and pulled out of the driveway.

"It's going to be okay, Seth," Tessa said, her fingers brushing his shoulder in reassurance.

"Isn't that supposed to be my line?"

"It seems like you might need to hear it more than I do right now."

"I told Julia that everything was going to be okay before I was deployed," he muttered, the memory one he'd tried to bury. Like so many others, it had been impossible to forget. "We'd moved from Virginia to Texas, and she was nervous about being so far away from home while I was overseas. I told her everything was going to be okay. It wasn't." He glanced at Tessa, trying to smile to take some of the sadness out of the words.

Her hand slid from his shoulder to his nape, her palm warm against his skin. "You didn't fail her. What happened was completely out of your control."

"Maybe so, but after her death, I promised myself that I'd never fail someone I cared about again."

"That's not the kind of promise you could ever hope to keep, Seth. Nothing is ever really in our control, and we can't know when we're going to be needed or by whom."

"Wise words, Tessa. My head knows it, but my heart is telling me that I can't fail you."

"You never could." She brushed her fingers along the back of his neck. He grabbed her hand and squeezed gently, his heart beating wildly for her.

He hadn't realized how much he'd needed this, had forgotten how nice it felt to be heading to church with a woman he was crazy about by his side. His life had been too full to ever be empty, but his heart had had a place that needed to be filled. God had seen that even if Seth hadn't.

"Here's what I'm thinking, Tessa," he said as he pulled into the church parking lot. "Pumpkin and apple pie."

"What?" She laughed, probably not expecting him to start talking about pies.

"For Thanksgiving this year. Next year, we'll fly to the East Coast and stay at my folks' place. Then Mom can cook for us."

"You're making a lot of plans for the two of us."

"Does it bother you?"

"I...don't think so."

"We'll work on that," he replied, lifting her hand, pressing a kiss to her knuckles.

She flushed and tugged away, a half smile hovering on her lips. "We're going to be late."

"Stay there. I'll come around." He jumped out, scanning the full parking lot. The day felt alive again, a few birds swooping low over a nearly bare cherry tree. The police cruiser sat near the entrance to the lot, and the officer waved as Seth rounded the truck.

A normal morning, but Seth still felt something in the air. A whisper of danger. A hint of trouble.

He couldn't ignore it any more than he could ignore the need to protect Tessa from it.

Please, God, don't let me fail her, he prayed as he helped her out of the car and escorted her into church.

NINETEEN

Being at church felt like spending time with an old and very dear friend.

Being there with Seth felt like every dream Tessa had ever had coming true.

It felt like family and forever, and she couldn't stop thinking about that as she sang hymns and listened to the pastor speak of faith in tough times.

She'd had plenty of tough times, but she wasn't so sure about the faith part. She'd been so tentative, so unsure. She wanted more, though. She wanted the sure and confident faith that Seth seemed to have.

He took her hand as the final chord of the final hymn faded away. "Let's sneak out before a hundred people converge on us."

"Why would they?"

"Curiosity?" He smiled, his eyes the warm blue of the spring sky. "You know how these things work."

Not really. It had been a long time since she'd been part of a church community. She hadn't realized how much she'd missed it until just now. This was where she wanted to be on Sunday mornings—in church, next to Seth.

She let him tug her through the exiting crowd.

They walked into the parking lot surrounded by a community of believers, the throng of people comforting rather than disconcerting. For the first time in what seemed like months, Tessa felt relaxed and at ease.

She got into Seth's truck, humming the last hymn, excited and happy and so ready for whatever the future would bring. She couldn't believe the way she was feeling—it was as if someone has switched on a light in her soul.

"You're glowing," Seth murmured, his fingers trailing down her arm.

"I'm happy."

"It's a good look on you, Tessa. Stay that way." He winked and closed her door.

She wanted the moment to last. She wanted the past to be washed away, the present and the future to be all that mattered.

She wanted to believe that God had brought her to this place, and that He planned to keep her there, safe and happy and secure.

"You're quiet," Seth pointed out as he maneuvered through the parking lot.

"Just thinking."

"About?"

"How fleeting a moment is, and how much I don't want this one to end."

"Every moment ends."

"I know, but I don't want any of this to end." She waved her hand at the November landscape, the golden fields and grazing horses, the mountains already tipped with snow, towering in the distance. "Pine Bluff. The people in it. *You.* I want it to last forever, Seth, but that's not the way life works."

"Sometimes it does." He took her hands and kissed

her palm. She closed her hand into a fist, holding onto the warmth of his lips.

Maybe he was right. Maybe it could last. Maybe five, ten, fifty years from now, she'd still be living in Pine Bluff, still be riding home from church with Seth beside her.

Dreams were so easy to believe in if she let herself.

Seth's cell phone rang, and he answered, murmuring a few words that she could barely hear. When he was finished, he shoved it in his pocket, and met her gaze.

"Change of plans. We're going to have to skip lunch."

"What's going on?"

"Remember the print Logan pulled from your back door?"

"Yes."

"Logan found a match."

"Who is it?" she asked, her mouth suddenly dry and hot, her head throbbing with tension.

She already knew what he was going to say. She just didn't know if she could handle hearing it.

"Andrew's."

His name landed on her like a physical blow that stole her breath. "Are they sure?"

"Logan petitioned to have his juvenile record opened. His prints were in it. They're a match."

"Andrew is alive." She breathed the statement more than spoke it, her heart tripping and jumping so fast she felt dizzy.

"Yes. Logan wants me to escort you to the station. He has a couple of photos for you to look at."

"What photos?"

"From footage taken at local convenience stores. He's been asking around, trying to find out if any strangers have been noticed in town. He took surveillance video from a couple of places."

"Why didn't he mention it before?"

"We can ask him that when we get there," Seth responded, his eyes on the rearview mirror.

"What's wrong?"

"Nothing."

"You're not acting like it's nothing."

"You know that I'm paranoid when it comes to protecting you, Tessa." He turned his attention back to the road, his jaw tight, his expression hard.

"You don't believe that and neither do I." She looked out the back window. The patrol car was several car lengths behind, Sunday-morning traffic filling the normally quiet country road.

"Things look okay for now, but I'm not banking on it staying that way. If Andrew is alive, he's spent five years planning this. He isn't going to let anything get in the way," Seth muttered.

"Get in the way of what? Killing me? He could have done that dozens of times in dozens of ways if he really wanted to."

"He tried."

"What do you mean?"

"On the fifth anniversary of your husband's death. Remember?"

How could she not?

She touched her neck, remembering hard fingers and whispered words. "We don't know that that was Andrew," she said, not believing what she was saying even as she said it.

"Who else could it be?"

"Anna? Someone else?

"You're grasping at straws. All the evidence points

to Andrew, and we've got no reason to believe it's any-one else. After we meet with Logan, I'm bringing you back to the safe house. You'll stay there until Andrew is found."

"Says who?" she snapped, fear and anger roiling into a mass of feelings that she couldn't quite control.

"I'm not going to be the bad guy, here, Tessa. You're too smart to think you can keep living in your place while Andrew stalks you. Eventually, you'll be at the wrong place at the wrong time."

"What about Bentley?"

"I'll keep him until this is over."

"I thought you'd be at the safe house."

"I will be, but I'm not going to be working as a secu-rity agent. I'm too close the case, and I don't want my feelings for you to blind me to things that I should see." His honesty disarmed her, and her frustration slipped away.

"I'm sorry. I know you're just trying to help and—"

"I'm doing more than trying to help." He paused, glancing in the review mirror again and frowning. "I'm trying to keep you alive. Tessa," he said, taking his eyes off the mirror for a moment, "I'm falling in love you. I haven't made any secret of that."

Tessa's heart nearly stopped in her chest. She was afraid, afraid to give voice to what she was feeling. Afraid that if she did, Seth would be snatched away as quickly as Daniel had been.

"If you don't feel the same, I need to know it, Tessa."

Her heart opened to his words, but she couldn't get her mouth to do the same.

She had so much fear and worry, and she didn't want to be disappointed again. Heartbroken again.

Lost.

So many years spent wandering, trying to find a place that felt like home. She'd finally found it, but she didn't know if she could rise to the occasion and accept what she was being offered. She wanted to—she wanted to desperately. She wanted to give him what he wanted, to say the words that would seal whatever it was that was between them.

She just had to get them past the huge lump in her throat and the terror in her soul. "I—"

Seth swerved onto a side road, the movement so quick and unexpected that Tessa slammed into the door.

"Hang on!" he growled. "We've got a tail."

"What?" Tessa shifted to look out the back window, and then wished that she hadn't. A blue pickup barreled toward them, the windows tinted nearly black. "Where's the police cruiser?"

"Hopefully following. This guy is coming fast, Tessa. Get down and stay down until I tell you different."

"What about you?" she yelled as Seth pressed a hand to her upper back and forced her down.

"Stay down," he repeated, his voice eerily calm and quiet.

That scared her more than the pickup had.

She yanked her cell phone from her purse, dialing 911 as Seth swerved again and then came to a sudden stop. She flew forward, the belt tightening as her head slammed into the dashboard.

She saw stars, then felt a cold, crisp breeze.

Seth's door was open, the autumn air drifting in.

No sign of him.

A loud report shattered the silence, and Tessa screamed, cowering in the vehicle while Seth fought for his life and hers.

For a moment she was back in the village, children

screaming, women crying, guns firing. Fire and smoke and the coppery scent of blood in the air.

She gagged, crawling across the seat and tumbling out onto cold earth.

"Seth!" she screamed his name, her throat raw, her heart racing.

Please, God, please, let him be okay.

Please.

"I told you to stay down," he growled, slipping out from behind the open door, his hair ruffled, his eyes blazing.

He looked better than sunrise after a long dark night.

Better than spring on the frozen tundra.

He looked like hope and the future, and she wanted to throw herself into his arms.

"Get back in the car, Tessa!" he snapped, nearly shoving her backward as he turned to face the truck, a gun in hand.

"Is he alive?"

"I don't know, but I plan to find out!"

"Let the police handle it," she said, but she scrambled back into the truck.

"Just—" He never finished. The truck's window exploded just above her head. Another explosion rocked the air.

No. Not an explosion. A gunshot.

Something whizzed past her head, slamming into the seat a few inches from her face.

She screamed and was yanked backward, hard hands on her ankles.

"Get out. Get down!" Seth shouted, but he didn't seem to be willing to give her time to do it, either.

She was on the ground, face pressed to the dirt, Seth

covering her with his body before she realized what
was happening.

"Get out of the truck! Keep your hands where I can
see them!" someone shouted.

Tessa tried to raise her head to see who was speaking, but Seth pressed her back down.

"Don't. Move."

Tessa thought she caught a whiff of African heat and
warm blood. She gagged, and tried to take a deep breath
and clear her nose and throat. The scent was still there,
hanging in the air, swirling around her. Something fell
onto the ground beside her face, a drop of deep-red
blood that sank into the dry earth. She looked up at
Seth and tried to focus on him, tried to bring herself
back into the present. She wasn't in Africa. She wasn't
in the middle of the massacre. She was here, now, with
Seth. The man she loved.

"You're hurt," she gasped, shoving against Seth.

He didn't move. "We both will be if you don't hold
still."

His hand slid up beside her face, his gun aimed at the
truck. A police cruiser had pulled up behind it, an officer taking cover behind its open door, his gun drawn.

"I said, get out of the vehicle. Keep your hands where
I can see them." His words echoed through the air, and
the truck door opened. A man fell out onto the ground,
a gun clattering beside him.

"Hands where I can see them," the officer repeated,
his gun aimed at the man's head. "Nice and slow."

Slowly, the driver raised his hands, then his head.

He didn't look at the officer, though.

His gaze was on Tessa, his dark eyes as familiar
as Tessa's own, his scarred face one she would have
known anywhere.

"Andrew," she whispered, and he grinned, his eyes feral.

"Long time no see, sis," he responded, his voice raspy and hard.

"I thought you were dead." She tried to move, but Seth was a dead weight against her back, his gun hand steady near her face.

"Wished I was, you mean?"

"I would never have wished that," she replied truthfully.

"Of course not. You've always been too good for something like that." Andrew glanced at the officer who'd eased out from behind the door. "Too bad you called Jack, Tessa. We could have had a lot of fun together with what I made in Kenya."

"What are you talking about?" she asked, her skin crawling as he turned his attention back on her.

"You knew what I was doing. I realized that when that investigator from the board arrived and started digging into things."

"Anna?" She had no idea what he was talking about, and she pushed against Seth again to let her up.

"Don't act stupid! Yes, Anna. Little witch. I knew she was trouble when I picked her up from the airport. She kept asking questions about who was in charge of the books, who had access to our funds. Someone tipped the board off, and she was sent to find out what was going on."

"Jack said the accountants discovered that funds were being misappropriated. I never—"

"You did!" He spat the words out. "You knew, and instead of coming to me and giving me a chance to explain, you called the mission board."

"No, I didn't!"

"You did. We both know it. You forced my hand. Forced me to kill my own brother."

His words were so surprising she couldn't speak, couldn't think of one word to say that could make any difference.

"Nothing to say to that, Tessa? No defense?"

"You killed Daniel?" It was all she had, the only thought in her head.

"I hired men to stage my kidnapping. I paid them good money to help me disappear. They got a little carried away and started killing people. They probably would have killed me if I hadn't managed to bribe one of them into letting me go."

"Andrew..." She couldn't continue, couldn't speak past the horror.

"You and Jack and Anna, you caused all that death. You killed all those people. Now it's time for you to pay." He glanced at the police officer, then his hand dropped and he pulled something from behind his back.

A gun.

Pointed straight at Tessa's face.

She had a single moment of stark terror, and then the world exploded.

TWENTY

Seth fired once.

And again.

He felt a moment of satisfaction as Andrew's gun flew from his hand and he fell to the ground, blood pouring from his wrist.

"Keep your hands where I can see them!" The police officer hollered.

Andrew twitched but didn't reach for the weapon. He was done and he knew it. Finished with his bid for revenge.

"Sinclair! Drop your weapon!" The police officer shouted.

Seth did as he commanded, the tension in the air thick and heavy. Any unexpected movement and more bullets would fly—this time, in Seth and Tessa's direction.

"Don't move. Any of you," the officer continued as he frisked Andrew, finding a knife and a small handgun in a holster beneath his coat. He looked at Andrew's wrist, scowling at the blood bubbling up from the groove dug by Seth's bullet.

"You'll live," he pronounced and cuffed him, calling for an ambulance as he led him to his car.

Seth hadn't aimed to kill, but he'd been tempted.

Especially since Andrew had come prepared to finish what he'd started.

If Seth hadn't pulled over and shot out his tire, Andrew would have pulled up beside the truck and fired until he hit his target.

The knowledge burned like fire in Seth's gut. It was almost enough to distract him from the pain in his shoulder and the blood dripping out of it.

He'd made a rookie mistake, allowing himself to lose focus for a split second, and that split second had nearly cost him his life. It could have cost Tessa hers. He'd spend the rest of his life thanking God for the fact that the truck window had changed the trajectory of the first bullet. If it hadn't, she might be dead.

He shuddered, wanting nothing more than to drag Andrew from the police cruiser and teach him a lesson he wouldn't ever forget.

"That was a risky move, Sinclair." The officer threw the comment over his shoulder as he slammed the cruiser door and stalked across the space that separated them. "You should have waited until I caught up."

"He was closing in too fast, and I knew he'd be armed. He'd have caught up to us before you did, and once he started shooting, there was no telling what would have happened."

Seth stood, offered Tessa a hand up. She was pale, her freckles dark against her stark white skin, her eyes vivid green. A smudge of dirt marred her cheek and her palms were scraped from sliding across the dirt, but she was alive, unharmed. That was all that mattered.

"You still should have waited," the officer grumbled as another police car pulled in behind his.

"Like you waited to frisk the guy?"

"He was offering a stellar confession. I didn't want to interrupt."

"Your hesitation could have gotten Tessa killed," Seth snarled.

"Things were under control," the officer protested as Logan Randal jumped out of the police car.

He ran toward them, his expression hard and grim. "What happened?"

"We've got him." Seth gestured to Andrew.

Andrew's gaze was still on Tessa from behind the window of the car, his hatred palatable. It took every ounce of training and common sense that Seth could muster to keep himself from yanking the guy out of the cruiser.

"Looks like you took a shot in the process," Randal said.

Seth shrugged, pain shooting through his shoulder. Not the best place to be shot, but at least it hadn't hit something vital. "I'll live."

"You've been shot?" Tessa gasped, her gaze dropping to his coat and the blood seeping through it. "You need to sit down."

"You worry too much," he murmured, pulling her into his arms. She fit perfectly there, her hands resting on his waist, her head tilted so that she could look into his eyes.

"You don't worry enough. At least, not about yourself." She slid an arm around his waist and led him toward the truck. "Sit down. Let me look at your shoulder. We need to try to stop the bleeding while we're waiting for the ambulance."

"I'm fine." But he could feel that she was right—blood was pulsing out with every heartbeat.

He settled on the driver's seat and allowed Tessa to

ease his coat off. She smelled like sunshine and summer rain, and if his arm had been cooperating, he'd have pulled her closer.

It wasn't.

His brain wasn't cooperating, either. His thoughts were muddy and muted, his movements sluggish as he brushed her hand away from his shoulder. "Let the doctor deal with it."

"If it isn't dealt with now, you're going to bleed to death," Tessa muttered, her hand shaking as she pressed the sleeve of Seth's coat to the wound.

"I'm not going to bleed to death." He covered her hand with his, trying to still her trembling.

"You're in shock. You don't know how badly you're hurt." Her voice broke, and a single tear slipped down her cheek. He slid his good arm around her waist and tugged her down so she was resting on his knee. She balanced there, one hand tentative on his uninjured shoulder.

"I'm not in shock, and I'm not that badly injured. I promise." He looked into her eyes and saw fear, worry and sadness.

"This is all my fault," she whispered, her voice raw with emotion.

"None of it is your fault. Andrew is nuts. He's not worth being upset over," he said.

She nodded, but another tear escaped.

"Why are you crying?" He brushed the tear away, his palm resting on her cheek. His shoulder throbbed and his thoughts were muddled, but his love for her was as clear to him as daylight.

"Because I'm the reason Daniel and all those people died, and all I can think about is how much I don't want to lose you."

"You aren't the reason, Tessa. Andrew is. And you're not going to lose me," he promised as an EMT edged in.

"Ma'am? Can you step to the side and let me take a look?" the dark-haired man said, his hazel eyes filled with compassion.

Tessa didn't want to move. She was so afraid that she'd walk away and never see Seth alive again.

"Go on. I'll be okay," he whispered, kissing her gently.

She nodded and did what she'd been asked to do, moving to the side, watching as the EMT pressed gauze to Seth's wound. Within minutes, he was on a gurney, being wheeled into the ambulance.

She followed, anxious to be beside him again.

"I'm sorry, ma'am. We don't have room in the ambulance. You'll have to follow us to the hospital," the EMT said as he climbed into the ambulance and closed the door.

The engine roared, sirens blared, and Seth was gone, carried off to a hospital that was supposed to be able to keep him alive.

Go on. I'll be okay, he'd said.

Would she remember those words the way she'd remembered Daniel's last words to her?

Would they fill her mind as she worked, ran, went about her days?

Please, God, let him be all right. Please, don't take him from me when I just finally found him.

The prayer welled up from the depth of her heart, spilling out with all the desperation she felt. She'd been so close to having everything she'd ever wanted. So close to believing that her dreams would come true, that she really would have the desire of her heart.

Would it be snatched away again?

Have a little faith.

The words seemed to come from nowhere and everywhere.

Seth's words.

God's words.

Her words.

All mixed up and jumbled together into that one thought.

Have a little faith that things will work out. That whatever happens, I will move forward with life, finding a way to make the best of what I have.

She'd nearly lost what faith she'd had when Daniel died. Slowly, she'd begun to grasp it again.

Or maybe, it had been thrust at her.

Maybe God had gotten tired of her fumbling attempts to draw closer to Him, and He'd dragged her in, pulled her back, shown her once and for all that He was there, just waiting for her to realize that He had always been as close as a prayer.

She wiped away tears. She was done crying. Done mourning for what she'd lost. God had given her what she needed. *More* than she'd needed. She was going to make the most of it, enjoy every minute of it. Live in the present rather than the past.

Be happy for the moment rather than worrying about what would happen when it ended.

"Are you okay?" Logan touched her shoulder, his hard face soft with concern.

"I need to get to the hospital," she replied.

"I'll have someone take you there." He motioned for a uniformed officer who was exiting his patrol car. "Nate, can you give Tessa a ride to Sacred Heart? I'll meet you there after I have a little talk with our perp."

"Sure," the officer smiled. With a shaved head and a

tattoo peeking out from the collar of his uniform shirt, he looked more like a gang member than a police officer. But his smile was warm and his hand gentle as he steered Tessa toward his car.

"Your friend is going to be just fine," he said as she slid into the passenger seat.

"I hope you're right," she murmured.

"Have a little faith, ma'am," he responded, offering a quick smile as he closed the door.

Coming out of anesthesia stunk.

Seth had been through it enough times to know exactly how it felt, but that didn't make it any more pleasurable.

He reached for a glass of ice water on the table beside the bed, wincing as the stitches in his shoulder tugged and pulled.

"Let me do that for you, Mr. Sinclair," a pretty nurse offered, her quick smile doing nothing to cheer Seth.

"I'll manage," he grumbled, taking a sip of the water to wash away the remaining sting of the intubation tube. Thick bandages covered his shoulder. He hoped that meant that the surgery to remove the bullet had been successful.

Seth figured he should be happy about that, but aside from the nurse, the room was empty, and that wasn't what he'd been hoping for when he'd opened his eyes.

"Is there anything else you need?" The nurse fiddled with the IV pole next to the bed.

"Yeah. I need Tessa."

"Who?"

"Tessa Camry. Can you see if she's around?"

"I'm not sure the doctor wants you to have visitors

yet. You're still in recovery. Once we wheel you down to your room—"

"That's fine." He sat up, his stomach heaving—a side effect of anesthesia that he knew well and hated. He ignored it. "I'll find her myself."

"You need to lie down. You just got out of surgery."

"I'll lie down after I make sure that—"

The door opened, the scent of summer sunshine drifting in. Tessa. He knew it before he saw her, and his pulse picked up in response.

She stepped through the door, her gaze settling instantly on Seth. Her hair was a wild halo around her head, and she still had that smudge of dirt on her cheek. She was the most beautiful thing he'd ever seen in his entire life.

"What's going on?" Tessa asked, gazing at Seth who looked as if he was about to stand up and bolt from the room.

"I was just coming to find you."

"You shouldn't be going anywhere." Tessa crossed the distance between them, her heart aching as she looked at Seth's pale face, the thick bandages on his shoulder, the IV dripping fluids into him. "You just got out of surgery."

"That's what I told him, but I think he was pretty determined to find you." The nurse smiled. "Since you're in here, anyway, you may as well stay. Just try to get him to lie still. The doctor spent a lot of time stitching up the wound. We don't want him to open it back up again."

She walked out of the room, and Tessa turned her attention back to Seth. He was sitting on the edge of the bed, his face pale, his jaw dark with a five-o'clock shadow. He looked better than good—he looked like home and forever and all the dreams she hadn't dared to dream.

He also looked as if he was about to fall over.

"Don't even think about standing up," she warned.

"Is that any way to talk to a guy who is convalescing?"

"It is when he's about to undo everything the doctor just did."

"In that case, I guess I'll lie down." He settled back onto the pillow. "I have everything I was going to look for, anyway," he murmured.

She tugged the blanket up over his legs and leaned down so she was close to his ear.

"Me, too," she whispered.

"I hope you mean that," he replied, his good hand sliding along her arm. She felt his touch in her soul, felt a yearning so deep that she couldn't deny it. When she was with Seth, she knew that she was exactly where she belonged. When she was with him, she felt like the best of herself, the most of who she could be.

"I do," she responded, and she meant it completely, meant it forever.

"Good," he murmured, tugging her down, sealing the words with a kiss that shook her to her core.

She broke away, breathless and flushed, her heart beating hard for him. "I don't think the doctor would approve."

"I don't think I care," he said, and tried to pull her back.

She brushed his hand away, a thousand butterflies taking flight in her stomach as she looked into his eyes. "Thanksgiving is only a couple of weeks away. I don't want to do all the cooking myself, so you have to be better by then."

"You're planning to cook?"

"If you want me to." Tessa pulled a chair over and sat next to the bed.

"I want whatever you want, Tessa. I always will," he said softly, his words so sweet and so beautiful that Tessa's eyes filled with tears.

"It's not that easy, Seth."

"It will be as easy as we allow it to be." He kissed her hand, his lips warm, his hand cool, his heart shining from the depth of his eyes.

She saw the future there, a future she hadn't been looking for, hadn't expected, but that she'd hold on to for as long as God allowed it.

She wove her fingers through his, her heart full of love and hope. "How about you rest and get better so we can work on the rest of forever together?"

"I have a better idea," he murmured, tugging her from the chair with a surprising amount of strength for a man who had just had surgery. "How about we start working on forever together right now?"

And, before she could protest, before she could think of one reason why it wasn't a good idea, he sealed the deal with a kiss.

* * * * *

Dear Reader,

I've had more than a few fans of the Sinclair brothers ask when I planned to tell Seth Sinclair's story. I finally have! A widower, Seth is working as a bodyguard and trying to dodge his family's matchmaking schemes. Physical therapist Tessa Camry is his perfect match. Strong and independent, she's a widow with a secret. One that just might get her killed. Neither is looking for a second chance at love, because neither expects to ever find one. But, there are no limits to what God can do, and as the two fight a hidden enemy, they discover that love is just as wonderful the second time around.

I hope you enjoy reading their story as much as I enjoyed writing it! And, I hope that whatever second chances you need, you will find them as you seek God's perfect plan for your life.

Blessings,

Shirlee McCoy

Questions for Discussion

1. Tess Camry was a missionary to Kenya. What led her there?

2. What are some of Tessa's regrets regarding her time in Kenya? What things do you think she would change if she could?

3. Have you ever thought you were following God's will but found yourself in difficult or trying times? How did you react?

4. Describe Tessa's relationship with Daniel. How was it affected by his brother Andrew?

5. Seth Sinclair was injured during a military tour, but the pain of that was nothing compared to the pain of losing his wife. How did that impact his life?

6. How big of a part does Seth's tight-knit family play in his life?

7. Tessa has been running for a long time, never really finding a place where she wants to plant roots. What is it about Pine Bluff that makes her want to stay?

8. Tessa has kept a secret for years. What is it and why did she keep it? Do you agree with her reasons for keeping the secret? Would you have done the same? Explain.

9. Seth loved his wife, and he doesn't think he'll ever meet anyone that he can connect with in the same way. How is that belief challenged after he meets Tessa?

10. I have heard it said that God is the God of second chances. What second chances have you had in your life?

11. Do you think that a person can have only one great love in his or her life? Explain your answer.

12. What are the commonalities that make it easy for Tess and Seth to connect?

COMING NEXT MONTH
from Love Inspired® Suspense
AVAILABLE AUGUST 6, 2013

HIDE AND SEEK
Family Reunions
Lynette Eason
Years after her daughter's abduction, skip tracer Erica James has a new suspect—Max Powell's missing sister. Together Erica and Max search for answers, but the kidnapper will do anything to keep them from finding Erica's daughter—including murder.

SHOCK WAVE
Stormswept
Dana Mentink
After an earthquake rips through San Francisco, Trey Black and Sage Harrington are trapped in an abandoned opera house—but they're not alone. A killer is with them, desperate to keep a secret buried.

DANGEROUS WATERS
The Cold Case Files
Sandra Robbins
Determined to solve her parents' murders, Laura Webber becomes a target herself. When she teams up with her ex-fiancé, cold case detective Brad Austin, to investigate, it's clear the killer knows their every move—and is closer than they ever imagined.

FATAL INHERITANCE
Sandra Orchard
After inheriting a remote farmhouse, Becki Graw finds that strange things begin happening to her. Can she and her handsome neighbor, police officer Joshua Rayne, uncover who's determined to drive Becki away before she loses everything?

Look for these and other Love Inspired books wherever books are sold, including most bookstores, supermarkets, discount stores and drugstores.

LISCNM0713

REQUEST YOUR FREE BOOKS!

2 FREE RIVETING INSPIRATIONAL NOVELS PLUS 2 FREE MYSTERY GIFTS

Love Inspired®
SUSPENSE

YES! Please send me 2 FREE Love Inspired® Suspense novels and my 2 FREE mystery gifts (gifts are worth about $10). After receiving them, if I don't wish to receive any more books, I can return the shipping statement marked "cancel." If I don't cancel, I will receive 4 brand-new novels every month and be billed just $4.74 per book in the U.S. or $5.24 per book in Canada. That's a savings of at least 21% off the cover price. It's quite a bargain! Shipping and handling is just 50¢ per book in the U.S. and 75¢ per book in Canada.* I understand that accepting the 2 free books and gifts places me under no obligation to buy anything. I can always return a shipment and cancel at any time. Even if I never buy another book, the two free books and gifts are mine to keep forever.

123/323 IDN F5AC

Name	(PLEASE PRINT)	
Address		Apt. #
City	State/Prov.	Zip/Postal Code

Signature (if under 18, a parent or guardian must sign)

Mail to the **Harlequin® Reader Service:**
IN U.S.A.: P.O. Box 1867, Buffalo, NY 14240-1867
IN CANADA: P.O. Box 609, Fort Erie, Ontario L2A 5X3

**Are you a current subscriber to Love Inspired Suspense books and want to receive the larger-print edition?
Call 1-800-873-8635 or visit www.ReaderService.com.**

* Terms and prices subject to change without notice. Prices do not include applicable taxes. Sales tax applicable in N.Y. Canadian residents will be charged applicable taxes. Offer not valid in Quebec. This offer is limited to one order per household. Not valid for current subscribers to Love Inspired Suspense books. All orders subject to credit approval. Credit or debit balances in a customer's account(s) may be offset by any other outstanding balance owed by or to the customer. Please allow 4 to 6 weeks for delivery. Offer available while quantities last.

Your Privacy—The Harlequin® Reader Service is committed to protecting your privacy. Our Privacy Policy is available online at www.ReaderService.com or upon request from the Harlequin Reader Service.

We make a portion of our mailing list available to reputable third parties that offer products we believe may interest you. If you prefer that we not exchange your name with third parties, or if you wish to clarify or modify your communication preferences, please visit us at www.ReaderService.com/consumerchoice or write to us at Harlequin Reader Service Preference Service, P.O. Box 9062, Buffalo, NY 14269. Include your complete name and address.

LIS13R

SUSPENSE

RIVETING INSPIRATIONAL ROMANCE

Years after her daughter's abduction, skip tracer Erica James has a new suspect—Max Powell's missing sister. Together Erica and Max search for answers, but the kidnapper will do anything to keep them from finding Erica's daughter—including murder.

HIDE AND SEEK

by

LYNETTE EASON

Available August 2013 wherever
Love Inspired Suspense books are sold.